PIOUS SECRETS

PIOUS SECRETS

IRENE DISCHE

BLOOMSBURY

Originally published as *Fromme Lügen*
Copyright © 1989 by Irene Dische

This edition first published 1991
Copyright © 1991 by Irene Dische
The moral right of the author has been asserted.

Bloomsbury Publishing Ltd, 2 Soho Square, London WIV 5DE

A CIP catalogue record for this book
is available from the British Library.

ISBN 0 7475 0835 6

10 9 8 7 6 5 4 3 2 1

Phototypeset by Hewer Text Composition Services, Edinburgh
Printed in Great Britain by Butler and Tanner Ltd, Frome and London

At the New York City morgue, a young forensic pathologist, Dr Ronald Hake, believes that secret sinning, like any disease, can be detected, dissected and treated. He wants to test his methods on a living patient, Carl Bauer, an elderly man he believes to be Adolf Hitler in hiding.

It is the 1950s, Hitler, alias Carl Bauer, appears a pious Catholic, a staunch American patriot with a German accent. He is tyrannical, smacks his grandchildren when he catches them reading books about the Third Reich, hates Jews, and is obviously lying about why and how he left Germany. His pretty daughter Connie is Hake's colleague at the morgue, the only female pathologist there, and Hake is mad about her. But she is as evasive about her past as her father.

A large cast of characters joins the moral chase, including Connie's ex-husband – a Jewish Nobel-Prize biochemist; a priest interested in just-war theory; and eventually the police.

Dedicated to M.R.D.

The North Wind shall blow
And we shall have snow
And what will poor Robin do then, poor thing?
He'll sit in the barn
And keep himself warm
And hide his head under his wing, poor thing!

1

God wanted us to study disease by His own freely available light, said the Chief Medical Examiner of New York City. He designed the City Morgue's autopsy room with two-storey high windows and a skylight, the dissection tables as tiny beds below. Within weeks the panes were so filthy that natural light went elsewhere. Summer came, the summer of the early fifties, without air-conditioning or two-storey screens. The flies took advantage each time some poor stifling pathologist inched open a window. The flies vandalized the morgue. One night the glass in the skylight crashed down into the autopsy room. That was shortly before Connie Bauer began spending time there, but the lesson resounded long after a steel plank was hammered over the skylight: God doesn't like theories about Himself and dissection.

Connie Bauer, MD, was a blonde with a bosom so maternal she could not see her feet from a standing position. She developed a peculiar dissection style, hunching her back and pulling in her stomach, reminiscent of a cat standing on her hind legs to play with a ball of string. Everyone adored her. The secretaries favoured her dictation because of her cute German accent. The other pathologists were grateful to see a live female at the morgue. They liked to copy her 'pussycat' style at the table and declaim that it was not easy.

The pathologists all knew each other's cutting techniques. Dr Miele enjoyed a good cigar while he worked, and he was so tall that he could reach everything from a sitting position. The way he swung his surgical instruments, the cigar clenched between his teeth, the way he said 'innachural cu–oses', earned him the nickname 'Broadway Butcher'. Dr Guttenberg was small and powerful. He had a way of squinting and calculating at a cadaver's side. He was considered an excessively even-tempered man, but one night, when everyone else had gone home leaving him alone to finish an autopsy, he smeared four-letter words on the blackboard in blood.

Dr Hake was that day's intellectual at the City Morgue, a handsome, stand-offish pipe-smoker in his mid-thirties with hair the rich colour of burgundy sauce. He had volunteered to take the smallest, shabbiest office because he found the view so romantic: affixed to the wall outside, and always readable from his window, was the sign 'Mortuary'. He spent most of his salary and all of his emotions on writing books about life and its meaning, couched in the medical prose he admired. He had more recently attempted a poem. This had created quite a sensation; it was about organs. He was the only member of Pathology who professed to know that inside man lay not only insides, but also a soul, and that inside each soul was a dirty secret. This made him frown a lot, which contributed, along with his rate of publication, to the awe the secretaries felt for him.

Dr Bauer, at twenty-eight the youngest member of the staff, enjoyed Pathology. It gave her the chance to have the last word on what the other doctors, and in particular the happy-go-lucky surgeons, had been doing. She neither minded nor really noticed that she was the only woman on the service. She dressed carelessly, in men's shirts and wide skirts. Her favourite companion was her eight-year-old daughter, Sally, whom she liked to take everywhere with her. As a consequence, Sally was another regular at the morgue. Her mother often fetched her and her nine-year-old brother Dicker from school in the afternoons and, after she put Dicker on a bus home alone, took Sally to the hospital and made her wait in the secretaries' office while she finished a case. Alice and Blessed, the elderly Jamaican secretaries, doted on the small, messy child, and spent their time trying to tidy her. 'Your hair has gone off,' they scolded, which sounded morbid in that environment.

Sometimes Sally brought her violin along, and the secretaries let her practise in the specimens office. The scratching of her fiddle was audible down into the autopsy room. This was before the spread of Muzak, and the pathologists' ears were not scarred and indifferent to musical pain. Sally's playing made them work faster, chopping instead of cutting, stabbing instead of inserting. Sally's music had quite the opposite effect on Dr Bauer. It put her into a trance of satisfaction, slowed her down, made her smile at her colleagues.

One Monday afternoon something unusual happened. Dr Bauer was dissecting a decomposed cadaver with Dr Hake, when Sally's rendition of the chorale from the Ninth Symphony penetrated the autopsy room. Dr Bauer smiled. Dr Hake took the smile personally. His mouth gave a smack breaking the suction of his usual frown to return the smile. Then the smile stuck to his face for the longest time, despite the stench.

*

3

On the morning before this exchange of smiles, Sally's father called Connie and said, 'Sally told me Saturday that you've been taking her to the City Morgue. That is not a place for children.'

Connie replied, 'Nor is your bedlam the place for children. I heard about the wine bottle in the paper bag you took to see *Snow White*. And about the little magazines hidden in the back of your bookshelf.' Connie only spoke with candour to subordinates, a pool of three individuals – two children and the adult she called her 'ex-hosband', a chemist named Stanislav.

Stanislav Reich had walked out on Connie a year before. He had not meant to. The family was taking a Pullman trip through the West. Seeing America was part of Connie's agenda for becoming part of America. Stanislav felt this was sheer expense. He said Connie was a sucker, falling for the Discover America pitch that sounded all winter on the radio. He repeated his objections for weeks after she volunteered for the weekend autopsy service in order to pay for the trip herself. 'Żoker!' shouted her husband in his Polish accent. 'Jórę żoker!'

But he couldn't prevent her from booking a family compartment to Salt Lake and back. 'To the middle part!?' he cried. 'Out there it's a quicksand of comics and ringdings.'

Perhaps the divorce should be blamed on the porter who told his passengers they were reaching the middle of America in the middle of the night. The coincidence infuriated Stanislav; he could not sleep. Back in sensible Stockholm, one was putting up names for the Nobel Prize. He let himself out of the family compartment and tried to pace the gyrating halls. When the train made an unexpected stop at a small town, he climbed down to see if he could walk off his anger on solid ground.

4

The train pulled away as he was already miles into a cornfield.

When Connie returned to Manhattan she took her suitcases up to their shabby uptown apartment with its expensive view of the Hudson. Instead of unpacking, she added more clothes to the cases. Stanislav watched, a frail, untidy figure, his large features arranged in an expression of horror. She unpacked them on the other side of the view, in her family's New Jersey house, while her father, porky, neat Carl Bauer, watched with the same horrified expression.

Connie began to refer to Stanislav as her 'Ex' long before she believed the separation was permanent. Ex didn't pay too much attention. His nomination to the Nobel Prize had come through. When the prize went to someone else, he missed Connie briefly. He looked for someone to replace her, and since he wasn't fussy, he found someone quickly. When this one got away as well, he bought himself magazines. A year passed, and Ex's name was said to be high on the Nobel Prize list for chemistry again.

He found it a bother looking after the children on Saturdays, but he had to insist on it. When Sally regaled him with descriptions of the morgue, he panicked. She could pick up dangerous germs there, carry them (she was much too tough to come down with anything herself) and infect him before his canonization.

Residual affection is hard to scrub off. Connie's marriage to Stanislav had been fiercely opposed by her mother. That is why she married him. After her mother died, it became possible to admit that the union was a failure, but even as a failure, her marriage fulfilled her dwindled emotional needs.

By impugning the morgue, Stanislav identified himself

with the aggressor, her mother, who had always referred to the morgue as 'your stink shop'. Connie began to hate him. Her emotions stirred up, climbed high and then drizzled down, charged particles that would attach themselves to anything.

When Dr Hake smiled at Dr Bauer, the late autumn afternoon sun appeared and warmed the red-brick morgue building. The elevator man suddenly felt the onset of a good mood. He drank the coffee his wife made him in a thermos and felt that life was worth living. The secretaries unpacked home-baked cookies in the typing room, and invited the pathologists to share them.

Practising her fiddle off in the specimens room, Sally felt tense. She wondered what her mother was doing. Her mother could not be doing much more than usual, finishing an autopsy. The tension in Sally grew, until it became a painful lack of concentration.

She placed her fiddle on top of a row of bottled foetuses and stepped out. The secretaries were typing in a battery, ears stoppered with headphones. They didn't see the child slipping by.

Sally entered the autopsy room before the smile on Dr Hake's face had set. From the threshold she had a view of her mother's back, the cadaver's torso, and Dr Hake from the front. His nose still showed the devastation left by a hormone storm in his teens. His cheeks were the colours of sunset, his mouth blazing with teeth. Then his mouth became a new moon, and the flesh around the edges turned grey.

Behind the autopsy table stood a bed covered with a sheet. A big toe poked out from beneath the sheet. It wore a tag.

Sally called, 'Mother!'

Connie turned. When she saw her child, she beamed. 'Come here, darling,' she said in a loud gay voice, 'I'll show you a heart. I want to prove to you once and for all that a heart looks nothing like a Valentine.'

At dinner that night, Connie didn't want to eat potatoes.

The potatoes were laid out in Meissen porcelain. Connie took the dish and passed it on to her father without taking any.

The housekeeper, Gerda, looked up from the end of the table. She glared. From the other end, Carl glared. Their eyes closed like pincers on Connie, who faced her plate.

'No potatoes, Connie?' said Gerda.

'Potatoes keep your feet on the ground,' said her father. He spoke with a German accent, crunching the marrow of his r's.

'My feet are sunk in quagmire, why do I need potatoes?' laughed Connie.

Carl's eyes spat. He stretched over the table to reach the porcelain dish. He heaped potatoes on to his plate. His anger pierced her, travelled on to pierce both children before soaring up to heaven as a prayer to his most merciful understanding God; please forgive my daughter her arrogant attitude towards new Kartoffeln.

The children looked at their sad, soft mother with her bountiful, soft body, suffering. They were afraid to look at Carl Bauer, whom they called the German name for grandfather, 'Opa', a word that rings with warmth and strength. He was an old source of apprehension, but also Generosity Incarnate, an Opa who took them in when Daddy did not prevent Mommy from leaving. He was

7

the source of heaviness in the family gene pool, a heavy man with heavy cheeks, cropped white hair and a white, clipped moustache. His hands were always newly washed, his expression rarely anything other than sad. The potatoes were firm, gleaming after hours of peeling. They required gratitude. Nine-year-old Dicker reached for the Meissen dish, and finished the last of them.

Connie was disgraced. She did not flee. 'Immer mit der Ruhe,' – keep your hat on – was her favourite expression. She stayed at the table through dessert, a labour-intensive lemon custard. She enjoyed two servings. She was used to disgrace.

'What did you do today, that your appetite for sweets is so good?' asked Carl.

'Two autopsies, Papa. Nothing extraordinary.'

'I'm afraid you're being evasive again.'

Gerda Schmidt and Carl Bauer traded sighs. Their sighs described the burden of taking on Connie's errors, in this case children. The immigration had been hard enough. They refused to talk about it. When people took their German accents as an excuse to ask where they came from, they replied, 'Cincinnati.'

They had arrived in Palmerston North in 1952, the new owners of a red-brick row house on River Avenue, an area washed in the evenings by the smell of sauerkraut. They came with little fanfare, in a small rented truck out of which they unpacked – so the neighbours reported – simple Sears-type furniture, and a bunch of old-fashioned sea-voyage trunks. No red and gold plastic recliner yet. They had a dachshund with them, the first in a dynasty of pure-bred chestnut-coloured longhaireds, which soon made Carl Bauer a common sight strolling patiently through the neighbourhood. He and his wife, a pretty middle-aged woman, spoke openly with the neighbours and the congregation at the local Catholic church, but told them nothing of interest. They said they had uprooted themselves from the Middle West because their only daughter Connie had become pregnant after starting her first year at college over in Manhattan, and they wanted to be near family. They expected to look after the grandchild when Connie continued to study. Everyone guessed that the child was illegitimate, and although it was soon said that the Bauers contributed very little to the basket passed around during mass, they were particularly popular at church because they were pitied.

The Bauers had already moved when they discovered that Connie had slotted her pregnancy for High Degree Evasion. She had not only lied about the pregnancy until it was visible. It transpired that she was also lying about who the father was (not a Stanley but a Stanislav), lying about his relationship to the Catholic Church (he had none; he was Jewish), lying about having moved out of the freshman's residence and in with Stanislav a good ten months earlier, after marrying him.

'I don't like to talk about certain things, because . . . they make me so sad,' said Carl Bauer. 'That's different from being evasive. I just want some peace and quiet in my old age, not suddenly a family of naughty children to look after.'

Gerda nodded and stared at the potato dish. She had refused help when her workload went from one to four persons. She simply ran her varicose limbs on triple time; her bad temper was her loud, steady motor. After meals she scraped together the leftovers for the dog, who was waiting for them in the kitchen, his tail flailing. A normal American family. The dachshunds were all named, one after the other, Happy.

Gerda always cleared the table alone. The children fled the prospect of a chore, mumbled 'homework' and bounded to their improvised room. Connie never helped with housework. She went to her father, kissed him on his sallow cheek. If she noticed the tears in his eyes, she chose to ignore them. She said, 'Papa. I have such a lot of work tomorrow. I'm exhausted. I need some rest.' He nodded; grimness had already replaced heartbreak.

Connie left the small dining room that opened to an ordinary small living room, with low ceilings, cheap Persian carpets and heavy purple drapes. The curtains were almost unnecessary since the rhododendron bushes surrounding the house had been encouraged to grow till they covered the lower half of the windows. As a result the rooms were terribly dark, and the Bauer home had the integrity of a body, closed off and heeding its own rhythm. The rough plaster walls were crowded with clocks, crucifixes, souvenirs of American landmarks, and Carl Bauer's own watercolour landscapes. The pulse of the clocks was audible everywhere.

Connie stood beneath a framed Bill of Rights to pull on an extra sweater, before retiring to an unheated front porch. This was her room. There had been no other alternative available in the small house; nevertheless, the porch with its rubber and metal garden furniture was meted out to her as punishment, and she accepted it as such. In the course of a year, she never tried to make it comfortable, she never even turned on the electric heater Gerda had smuggled in.

She retired to the porch after dinner, brushed her short,

10

curly blonde hair, and then settled down on the rubber porch sofa she accepted uncomplainingly as a bed, pulling a blanket over her head. After a minute, when the sofa had warmed up, she emerged, tousled, and began to read a book about Caligula. She loved historical novels.

The house television was never used these days. A framed picture of Eva, Connie's mother, stood on top, next to a candle. This was always lit, always replaced before it could burn out. For one year after her death, Carl had decreed, the television would not be turned on. When the time was up, he extended the ban for another year. After dinner, he and Gerda got down on their knees in front of the twenty-two-inch screen and prayed for Eva's soul. They prayed for the length of a normal television programme, without taking any breaks.

Gerda's knees were arthritic, but tonight she stood up first, and then tugged at Carl Bauer's arms until he arose too. He thanked her, an unusual courtesy on his part. She said, 'Ja, ja,' impatiently, tearfully. She had adored Eva. Afterwards she went to her room and prayed some more. Her room was hung with crucifixes still sporting last year's palms. When she had prayed enough, she sat down at her sewing machine and read a religious tract the Tower people had sold her at the supermarket.

Carl sat on the red and gold-rimmed plastic recliner that had arrived the day the children moved in. That first evening Sally had sat down on the arm of the chair to kiss her grandfather goodnight, and Gerda had pushed her off and said, 'Your grandfather has so little, don't damage that too. Never lean against it.' Carl leaned way back in it, reading the newest *National Geographic*.

His 'den' was occupied by the children. Camp-beds were

set up on either side of the mahogany desk where he often recalled writing his doctoral dissertation in architecture. Dicker kept his secret supply of Marvel Comix beneath the mattress, and when he lay down they crunched. He wallowed on his fat stomach, reading them. Sally had spent her allowance on the *American Inquirer* again. She adored morbid news, but this evening she read something that upset her. She snapped her fingers, closed her eyes, groaned, 'Please don't let it be true! This is a disaster.'

It was not Dicker's style to be curious about his sister, or about anything else. He kept the pages of his comic flapping the way a mouse turns a treadmill. He had read nothing else since the surprise ending of their Discover America trip turned out to be the suburbs. After Carl Bauer took over the leadership of the family, his first act in office was to remove the children from their expensive private school in Manhattan. He placed them in the Helpers of the Holy Souls in Weehawken. As long as Dicker was a fat, unsportly bookworm with a German accent – why couldn't he lose that German accent! – he should be in an environment where American virtues were cultivated. The private school in Manhattan was full of notions. Notions about talent. It was hard enough on poor Dicker having a scrawny intellectual for a father.

Dicker never complained, and comforted himself reading about Jughead, an even greater fool than himself, even if he didn't have a German accent. But his view of his comic was suddenly obstructed by Sally's *American Inquirer*. He read the headline. EVIDENCE THAT ADOLF HITLER IS HIDING IN THE USA!

'D'you think,' asked Sally, 'that it could be Opa?'

'Don't be ridiculous, dingbat. Opa? If Opa was Hitler

he wouldn't wear a moustache like that. It would give him away,' replied her brother. 'And besides, he's from Cincinnati. They all have German accents out there.'

'You're wrong. He's Hitler. It explains everything about this family. He moved to Cincinnati from Germany. And Hitler would never shave off his trademark. And he does hate Jews, especially Daddy.'

'That's because the Jews executed Jesus,' said Dicker.

'That's too long ago,' replied Sally, 'to matter. It's because they talk so much about money that Opa hates them.'

Two mornings after Connie proved to Sally that hearts don't look like Valentines, Connie felt hers pounding. She interpreted the feeling in her chest as instructions about what to wear. Instead of her regular outfit, she put on a pretty red dress. Her children felt alarm and revulsion as she cocked her head at the mirror, and smiled in an unnatural, formal way.

In fact, Connie's evasiveness was so chronic that it extended to herself. Her heart was grabbing for attention: she asked herself why and replied to herself, 'Because today is today.' The smile, however, was not deceptive. She was only trying to remember what she looked like when she was happy.

Then she remembered that today was Wednesday, and Dicker was scheduled to see a speech coach that afternoon, and then he was seeing a doctor about his girth. Connie felt optimistic about Dicker. Over breakfast, she pretended she had forgotten about his special activities, having resolved never, ever, to mention them. She told him Wednesday was a special day, a beautiful day to start something new.

Every act seemed unusual. The drive to school seemed long, Sally more garrulous than ever, and her remarks about her teachers rather ordinary and dull. Connie was frankly glad to drop them off. Very strange. Then she was suddenly gripped with a desire to see the hairdresser, whom she otherwise avoided, and ended up in his salon asking for a new perm. By the time she parked her grey Chevy in the hospital lot, she was late. She had never been late before.

The walk to her office was marked by irregularities. The morgue was at the far end of the hospital complex, across an alleyway from the psychiatric ward, only accessible by foot, and marked by the metal sign reading 'Mortuary' that swung in front of Dr Hake's window. It was ten in the morning by now, the patients on the male ward which faced the alleyway were finishing their milk and Ritz crackers. The music of a woman's walk on cobble alerted them.

Their tin plates clattered as they dropped them to rush to the windows. It was She, late today. They had watched for her earlier. But thanks to the hour, milk-break, they could give her a proper welcome now. Their feet thundered away again, returned, and they began to beat their cups against the bars. The patients on the upper floors heard the noise and joined in. This alerted those in cells facing the other direction. The building shook. No one can say what might have happened if the patients' banging had become rhythmic. Levitation, instant cure, Elysium. But they couldn't settle on a rhythm.

In the Department of Pathology one heard the racket and assumed the city was growing a new building somewhere. Everyone was glad Dr Bauer had finally arrived. 'Hi, Dr Bauer,' called Dr Miele. 'Hey, there, Dr Bauer, I've been waiting for you,' said Dr Guttenberg. Technicians sprang from different rooms, beamed at her, urged her into one room to look at a slide. When she returned to the corridor, another lay in waiting for her. 'Dr Bauer!' in gentle voices. 'We have a funny case, here, come and look.'

A while later her footsteps resumed, passing the elevator without pushing the button, on down another corridor where the harsh smell of formaldehyde grew strong, faded, and was replaced by the aroma of aftershave.

Dr Hake registered her approach after the footsteps didn't stop at the elevator. He began to sweat, and the sweat made him itch in places impossible to scratch. He stayed seated at his desk, surrounded by floating specimens in bottles. He re-read the title of his newest work, a study of the effects of piety on secrets, and dragged on his stately Bruyère pipe. He was going to draw on cases from the Medical Examiner's Office. He didn't know what exactly for yet. At the moment he hadn't gotten beyond a certain feeling he had when he read the title. Sometimes it was hard to concentrate. The desire to itch wagged inside his thighs, and along his scalp. Connie came into view. Blonde. That bosom, firm under white lab coat and white blouse, and then her very white skin. Her soft voice. He allowed his head to rise up like a bubble through a viscous fluid. She smiled at him easily, as if her visit meant nothing more than a visit.

'Come in, Dr Bauer,' he said, and put down his pen and removed his pipe.

She stepped in, without answering, still smiling. This means nothing.

He sighed.

15

She spoke: 'Juh hev so matsch tu du?'

Pearls to swine, your words, wine to water, yours to mine.

Hake eddied and spun like a leaf in the flood of his feelings, was carried to the source of the excitement, banged against it, held tight, and nearly drowned.

Connie was the upstart of the family, and therefore its most significant member. The others were extraordinarily affected by her. Like dependent clauses, their actions made sense but did not stand on their own.

'Dr Bauer . . . can I call you Connie?'

'Yes. And you're Ronald.'

'Connie.'

'Ronald'

Connie Ronald,

connieronald,

carnalnodney,

while Dicker was learning to stand straight, learning to pull in his stomach, while Dicker was learning about carbohydrate from a pamphlet.

while Sally at the Helpers of the Holy Souls was memorizing the numeration of sins mortal venial and all their subcategories.

while Carl Bauer was sitting at home in his plastic recliner, wrinkling his forehead about the naked pygmies in his *National Geographic*. There was an article about New Guinea natives wearing their penises in gourds.

while 'two pounds potatoes' met their peeler. Afterwards, Gerda ground them into powder, mixed them with water and leavening, and then pounded and kneaded their remains, forming them into balls. When the water was boiling in her biggest pot, she plopped them in,

while over in Manhattan, Stanislav mixed apple sauce with instant oatmeal, his favourite nutrition.

There was not much to the family – five family members including minors and the servant.

At this moment, all were restless. All thought of Connie.

'And what sin did you commit when you coveted your brother's marbles?' Sister Mary Angela asked.

Sally had a heavy library book on her lap, about great men in history, from Jesus to Eisenhower. One chapter was devoted to dictators. There were pictures of tsars, kings, and Hitler.

It was Opa, no doubt about it. She thought of her mother. She must be aware of this. It would cause her a lot of embarrassment.

Dr Hake and Dr Bauer approved of each other, in a frenzy,

while Carl's heavy body was dominating the springs of his plastic recliner. On days like this he kept it upright. On other days, when he was feeling more lazy than bitter, he lowered the chair, pushing a silver button on the side Down until it reached 'the ultimate recline'.

Today he couldn't sit upright enough. The springs lifted themselves in packs like dogs' noses. The clocks shuffled uneasily. Something was the matter. The curtains seemed poised for a wind. The candle in front of Eva's photograph stopped flickering and soared high. Carl Bauer rubbed his forehead. Nothing to blame on *National Geographic*. He never read the newspaper because he didn't like to work himself up about human beings, crime and politics. 'I've had enough of that in my life,' he grunted to Eva's portrait,

17

which showed Eva reclined on a lawn in a bright, flowered dress.

Gerda didn't hear that he was talking to Eva again. She was listening to her mutilated radio. Carl had broken the dial at the weather station to keep news out of the house. Partly cloudy and seasonally cold. She repeated this to the dog asleep next to the stove, switched off the radio and concentrated on the water bubbling around her dumplings. Hers – she felt everything in the kitchen was hers. She no longer collected a salary. She had voluntarily given up her two hundred dollars a month when the family moved to New York and began to complain about the higher cost of living. Without the salary she became, like an impoverished noblewoman who rouses guilt rather than resentment, socially powerful.

Eva had suffered under Gerda. The maid always called her Frau Dr Bauer, even when she cleaned her sick backside for her on the toilet. Eva, dying in a series of floral dresses, had watched Gerda cooking and realized Carl would enjoy the cooking for years to come. She looked at Carl's favourite dish, creamed spinach soup, and her penultimate thoughts were directed to the maid: 'I don't want another mouthful of that hideous stuff!'

Gerda repeated these words as she toiled over her dumplings. She could not make creamed spinach soup any more, although the children asked for it.

There had been no woman as kind as Eva, as suffering. Fate had turned against her for marrying Carl – Enough. Gerda poured the past from her thoughts, and refilled with worries about Connie. It occurred to her that Connie could marry again. And that, with her taste in men, it wouldn't be a handsome prince.

★

Stanislav slurped the apple sauce and oatmeal out of a cardboard bowl he had taken from the university cafeteria. The phone rang. It was Stockholm. He was anointed.

At the moment of triumph he lost interest in it. Lots of scientists before him and after him would win. The announcement came as an anti-climax. Now he had to go to Stockholm. And he hated flying.

Stanislav put down the receiver and finished his oatmeal.

Meanwhile Sister Mary Angela grabbed the history book from Sally's lap, and cried, 'What, may I ask, is this? So that's why you're not paying attention! Disobedience, and now probably Anger! You'll have a lot to tell Father Renard about. You'd better go and see him right away. Or you might die with your soul black as tar.'

Dicker snuck another potato chip out of the bag he had hidden in his briefcase. When the nurse came to fetch her pamphlet about carbohydrates, she found it covered with greasy fingerprints.

At the City Morgue, the secretaries began to wonder where Dr Bauer was. Dr Guttenberg wandered around looking for Dr Hake, whose office was locked. 'We have a post on a baby to do,' he grumbled. 'Looks like an abuse case.' The secretaries yawned and looked at the clock.

Dr Guttenberg returned to Dr Hake's office and heard the furniture dancing inside. He rattled the door knob and said, 'Dr Hake!' The furniture held still.

'Dr Hake, I know you're in there!'

But he couldn't prove it without opening the door. He rushed off to get the skeleton key from the super's office; Hake must have gone mad.

Hake had gone mad. He had made love to Connie on

19

his desk. He had never thought of using his desk for such a sport. It didn't seem right. Even worse, he hated having reservations in retrospect.

He walked around Connie as she sat in his office chair rolling her stockings up, and fastening them. Ingenious invention, garters. His interest in Connie began to pick up again.

'Do you want to come for dinner next Sunday?' she asked, as she wriggled back into her dress.

By the time Dr Guttenberg returned, Dr Hake's office door was open again, and he was engrossed in preparing a tattooed penis for the Medical Examiner's museum. Dr Guttenberg could scarcely complain about that, and it ruined his good mood for the day.

News of Stanislav's Nobel Prize confirmed Carl Bauer's dismal impression of his son-in-law. 'A prize. Certainly he manages a prize,' said Carl Bauer from his red and gold recliner. He craned his neck, and tried to loosen his tie. The dachshund dozing at his slippers sensed static, and looked up quickly. From the sofa the rest of the family watched the details of Carl Bauer's large, elegant hand wrenching at the knot around his neck. He glared at them, as if it was their fault that he couldn't undo it. Then he left it tight and said, 'Bah. I guess he'll hang on to the prize. A family is harder to keep. And good family life requires more work than chasing after prizes. He's lazy. That's a fact. He's a – '

'Oh Connie, Connie,' murmured Gerda, 'what have you done unto your Lord?'

' – and your children,' finished Carl Bauer. 'You undid everything I tried to accomplish. Marrying a – '

'After all he accomplished,' said Gerda. She had a way

of dropping a repetition into Carl Bauer's conversation just before he said an unkind word.

Carl Bauer closed his eyes to concentrate on his sorrow. There was no mistaking this for sleep; his eyes lay like trap-doors on the stage of his face. When they slammed open he had everyone's attention. He addressed his grandson. 'Dicker – learn from your father's bad example. Brains are not everything.

'And, by the way, good table manners count for a lot in life too. Please, *use* your napkin tonight. And be sure your mouth is empty when you speak at the table. Think of the animals. Do they talk with their mouths full? Dicker? Sally? Can you answer that?'

They cowered.

'No, they don't. Because it's not natural. Only Stanislav talks with his mouth full. In fact, he only talks when his mouth *is* full. And people give him prizes for his intelligence. They should see his table manners first. I don't want to be at that gala smorgasbord in Stockholm, when they'll regret having chosen him.'

'Speaking of which,' Connie said, 'I've invited a pathologist over next Sunday.'

2

Connie Bauer had Catholic reflexes: she associated God with good luck, bad luck, and dinner. Therefore it was only natural that she should invite a man to this formality whom she actually liked well enough not to introduce to her father. The purpose of the meal was to apply ritual like glue to an unsealed affair.

Just two Sundays after smiles had settled on our pathologists' faces, obscure and promising as doves, the Bauer family was pitched into unpleasant speculations. 'I've thought all along she wouldn't have left Stanislav if she didn't have some man lurking in the background,' Carl said to Gerda. 'Hiding in her emotional closet. That filthy, untidy place where she stashed Stanislav too, and how were we supposed to know?'

The Saturday night before the big event, Carl strode portentously to Connie's unheated porch (he hated going in there because, he said, Eva would faint if she knew the way Connie left all her underwear lying around). The children heard his footsteps all the way from their upstairs room and recognized the route. They didn't miss a confrontation between Connie and her father if they could help it, and ran for good seats in the doorway. She was sitting at a tin garden table doing her finger-nails. Carl had marched right up to her, his hands on

22

his hips, and was staring at her. She looked up languidly, aware that he had caught her busy at the sin of Vanity. The corner of his mouth rode up under the moustache when he asked, 'How long have you known Dr Hake anyway!'

She spat on the nail of her middle finger, buffed anew, and then held it aloft, the other fingers in a fist. She regarded her own middle finger, waved it ever so slightly in his direction, and answered, 'It's a new friend, I told you.'

'But you've talked about Dr Hake before,' said Dicker, sidling into the room. 'I remember the silly name. Last year.' He shivered in the cold. Connie made a point of noticing his shivers.

'That was another Dr Hake,' rejoined Sally. She stood next to Connie and put her hand around her mother's shoulder. 'This Dr Hake's just come.'

'And how was your speech therapy?' said Connie to Dicker, buffing her fingernails again. 'You never told me. Or how your overweight course last week for little fat boys went.'

The next afternoon Ronald Hake finally descended, into an atmosphere charged with expectation, hatred and fear. He was emotionally inexperienced in the role of catharsis, the son of self-centred, wealthy, pleasant people. They had spent their weak parental venom on the elder child. Ronald had learned early that the passions of important people were never directed towards him, and he had always provided emotionally for himself. This had made his relations to women adhere to simple laws: as soon as he felt their adoration, with its inherent requirement for reciprocity, he threw them out of his life. They threatened

23

like a revolution the established order of his feelings, in which he alone ruled.

Now in his affair with Connie he did not yet perceive any threat. Their time together was subject to so many external factors. At the hospital they were ruled by a junta of professional standards that had been in power for many centuries. Doctors could be slothful and wicked at home, but at work they were expected to be punctual, discreet, and willing to exhaust themselves. The patients of the forensic pathologists were never asked whether they felt repulsion ('horror magnus') at this final bit of hospital care, but their inability loudly to object did not make attending to them less urgent. New Yorkers were constantly succumbing to suspicious circumstances, and precise explanations interested not only the relatives but also the police and the insurance companies. Dr Hake had learned a lesson about professional conduct when he first started at the City Morgue and left a lower borough politician who turned green and died of drink out overnight in the autopsy room. The next morning, when Dr Hake returned to finish the post-mortem, he discovered the rats had gotten to the nose. Dr Hake's panic was answered by inspiration. He matched some green children's putty from the lobby Friendly Shop to the patient's skin colour and the public wake went off without a hitch. Since a pathologist's slip-up did not damage health so much as reputation and someone's wallet, it was really a very high-pressure job.

Dr Hake also knew that as soon as the day ended, Dr Bauer fell under the jurisdiction of her family. He had heard about her marriage 'failing' although gossip moved so slowly at the morgue that after Dr Bauer changed her telephone number in the secretaries' register, it took four full weeks for this simple fact to travel from Blessed to the

24

elevator man. Dr Hake assumed nevertheless that it would be difficult to assert a claim on Dr Bauer. In the first place, she was attractive. In the second, she refused to talk about herself. One had to assume that her estranged husband still meant a lot to her; after all, he was famous.

Ronald was conscious of the fact that Connie was as close as he would ever come to a Nobel Prize.

While Connie was surrounded by commitments, Ronald Hake rarely left his home, emotionally or physically. There were formal invitations, to be sure, to which he squired his tuxedo, his buffed Oxfords and his freshly loaded pipe. But Ronald had little need for human contact. He saw lots of dead people every day and this had always satisfied his need to socialize. When his only relative, an elder, unmarried sister, once irritated him about this, he swatted her with, 'Some of the most interesting people in the world are dead.'

At the morgue Dr Hake had trouble enjoying himself among the living. He avoided the secretaries, Alice and Blessed, because he felt guilty about the contempt he had for them. How often he wished that others weren't so terribly nice. Yet Connie's invitation to visit her at home came as a challenge to him, a normal Sunday dinner, with all those others contending for her affections, and so, in a spirit of competition, he looked forward to the event.

The day proved auspicious. He had departed from his tradition of having breakfast at a cafeteria. This ritual had been his substitute for Sunday mass ever since he started college. He always showed up when the doors opened at eight, crowded in with the others, jostled for a seat and waited in silence for the kitchen to open. When a bell rang, he shuffled along in the queue until he was abreast of the dispenser, and there was much satisfaction. Surrounded by people who wanted nothing from him, all going through the same motions, Ronald's brain roamed religion, politics, the arts, and now more recently the problems of bone reconstruction.

Three Sundays previously, in the middle of a congregation eating French Toast Special, he had jotted down the title of an essay about piety on the back of the sign 'Have a Good Day'. He believed in titles. Titles were not just candy wrappers; they were the head of the parade. Sometimes the floats were missing, and the marchers were lost among the onlookers. The title, 'The Effects of Piety on Secrets', was all he could grasp of a fleeting thought as it tore past, the suspicion that his room-mate at a Catholic boarding school, who had committed vile impurities with a hand-carved Madonna, might turn out more of a gentleman than himself.

He had lost his faith in organized religion at that school after hearing how expensive the tuition was. He had continued to go to mass, going through the motions, holding his hands in the steeple position, and admiring them like that, the strong, fleshy fingers in a position of exquisite symmetry, among the splayed ears and shorn occiputs of his comrades.

When Ronald realized that he no longer believed one could communicate with a Life Force by regular speech, he discussed this with a priest. The priest became excited. He assured Ronald that he'd been chosen to reach a higher plain of believing if he could communicate with God without actually chattering away. After this setback to his disbelief, the boy's scepticism took him a long time to formulate.

By the time he reached Princeton, he believed in a God

the Energy. The sacrament that brought one near Him was the exercise of thought and the pursuit of hard knowledge. He detested those who believed in any of the traditional metaphors of Catholicism, thought them superstitious. 'Superstition is a kind of hypochondria, paranoid mis-readings of physical signs. Stigmata everywhere.' Physical signs became Ronald's passion. He studied biology and then medicine, where Latin still meant something. He deemed operations preferable to miracles, and decided to become a surgeon. Then he opted for pathology, the better to know what was going on in invisible reaches. From medical school he sent his former room-mate nineteenth-century autopsy reports about cerebral–spinal disease in which onanism, 'as evidenced by the diseased state of the minute vessels', was listed as the cause of death.

Nothing irritated Ronald more than the absence of physical signs. He was aggravated that he could not read people's minds the way he read the insides of their bodies, and was suspicious of psychiatrists who said they could. He was certain that most people did not have gentlemanly thoughts, the way he did. Even his own strong feelings struck him as inherently amoral because they took com-mand. The enthusiasm of flesh for flesh short-circuited the power command in his brain, a kind of treachery. He blamed only himself for his passions, never the women who elicited them. 'It takes two to play baseball,' he said. His heart was really like a public square under the dictatorship of his head: patrolled by militia, surrounded by monuments, while off to one side the rebels were hiding in the houses. Every so often they got out. He did not bother to battle against the current rebellion because he knew he fully intended to allow the rebels run of the public square. They behaved childishly. Given the chance, they did nothing more than turn the square into a baseball field. Three home runs was the limit his brain tolerated. After that, he called off the game.

But while the game was in play, he was hopelessly unconcentrated. So the morning of his visit to Connie's home, he stayed home in bed thinking about sports. In the course of the morning he changed into a white suit, regarding himself for a while in his bathroom mirror. Hullo there, Yale Doctor. Losing his virginity had taken some doing, or, rather, undoing. He had disapproved of the Ronald that was a virgin because it showed a want of knowledge; it didn't tally with his self-image of dapper, controlled unavailability. But the only woman he knew very well was his sister, and she had outright refused him. Then he had tried an elderly secretary in the admissions office. Nix. He was too unromantic, she said, his name suited him too well. The way he complained about his inexperience as if it was a pimple she should cap for him. Go to a professional, kid. He had taken the train from New Haven all the way down to Washington, bought himself the classifieds and ordered someone to his hotel room. He had gone to the Capitol a boy, come back a man, etcetera. The way he placed his feet on the way back to campus, the step sending its vibrations along the leg muscles all the way up to the hip, registered everything. Wonderful, heady stuff, sex. But after that he knew what he was missing and didn't mind as much. For ever after, his reflection was his closest friend, someone he brushed his teeth with before going to sleep. His interest in Connie registered in his neglect of the mirror. And as the hour of his competition with her family approached, he completely forgot to wish himself goodbye, but departed with such a self-conscious bounce in his step that his hips churned.

He was going to have to take a bus to the suburbs. As a city man he did not even own a car. His one-bedroom apartment was just three blocks from the hospital. He knew if he had a car it wouldn't just be a Studebaker.

The bounce became less pronounced as he saw the weather. Cumulus wallowing over the city. The bus uptown had a shower in Harlem and arrived gleaming in the stettl of Washington Heights. He had to wait for another bus there, among a milling crowd of Orthodox Jews whom he regarded with something close to fear; he had never seen them alive before. They were the bane of the morgue, demanding immediate autopsies so they could get the relatives underground by sundown. Dr Hake had heard of their breaking and entering in order to wash their dead with the three gallons of water tradition required, and then dressing them before anyone could interfere, following stringent clothing rules that made no aesthetic sense, if you asked Dr Hake. No knots allowed in one's final garment, for example. But Dr Hake felt the Muslims were worse. They insisted that even during autopsy the faces of the dead faced east, which meant they ended up looking at traffic congestion on the East River Drive, as if that wasn't a metaphor for hell.

He began to enjoy the strange neighbourhood after he entered the safety of another bus, which soon left the city and deposited him in the familiarity of the suburbs. Now the fog turned over obligingly in its bed, and rolled off to sea.

The sky turned deep blue over Palmerston North, the afternoon sun poured over the red-brick houses, the bare black branches, slathered the empty white sidewalks. The strong, simple, patriotic colours of suburbia smelled of lawn and wet cement.

29

The Bauer residence was number 1207, in one of the many miles of streets that ran parallel to the river, each house with its parcel of lawn at the front and back, each with a staircase perched along the left shoulder, like a rifle. Ronald Hake, MD Yale University, was shocked. His own suburb had been spacious, individual, competitive, the houses highlighted their differences. At least number 1207 had made an attempt at something really novel: next to the mandatory front-yard willow stood a pole with a tin dachshund on top, which acted as a weather vane.

He pushed the doorbell, which piped the first three bars of 'Oh what a beautiful morning', and as the family inundated him, he held out the presents he had brought. Connie unpacked them, and wondered whether they were inappropriate: five (too many?) small boxes of chocolate (weren't flowers more usual?) with an inscription inside the top that read 'Get well soon – courtesy of the Friendly Shop' (free sample). She corrected herself: Ronald, of all people, would know what constituted a good manner.

His self-assurance had returned. He petted the doddering dachshund, enquired after his name, his pedigree and his age, before turning to the children. Dicker and Sally led the guest in, Dicker nicking his head as they passed beneath the crucifix in the front hall. Ronald Hake followed suit automatically. Thereafter, Dicker's head bobbed almost continuously. 'Oh, sacred heart of Jesus'; his lips rolled the mandatory words as though they were chewing gum. Crucifixes hung everywhere. Ronald imitated him, an abridged version, a hint of a nick. The members of the family noted the gesture and were amazed. Connie hadn't mentioned that the visitor was a Catholic. Nor that he had the courage of his convictions. Enough to nod at a crucifix. Too few people will die for their convictions, and even fewer will be embarrassed for them.

They respected also Ronald's size, the American shape: broad shoulders, a rolling walk, the pipe firm between his lips, and the vitality of his sauce-coloured hair. In an instant, the resentment at Connie's intruder changed to attraction. Gerda fled her feelings into the kitchen. Carl Bauer moved quickly too. He blocked Connie's path to Ronald, said, 'Let me show you around.'

Ronald spotted Connie in the distance, unmoving and alert. She was pleased that the connection between Ronald and her father had been made, and felt very feminine as the two men sauntered off. Only the dog dared to follow them, his tail high, but the master turned on him in public: 'That's enough, Happy. Dismissed!' and rapped the dog's snout. Happy furled his tail up to his belly, lamed his legs and dragged himself beneath the pine coffee table. Carl Bauer stared at him until he whimpered and tucked his nose between his front paws. 'He has become a nuisance,' Carl said. 'I told my granddaughter he can live another year. And my granddaughter said, "Another year? That's for ever!" She looked disappointed. She doesn't think too much of the elderly.'

Hearing her grandfather speak about her, Sally became the second family member to try and insinuate herself into this select group, attaching herself to Ronald's far side where Carl Bauer could not see her. Ronald ignored her, but did not denounce her. 'I collect *National Geographic*s, clocks and checker sets,' Carl Bauer said. 'I retired from my position as an architect when we left Cincinnati. But I always had hobbies, even as a young man. Then they were different. Although I still like to paint. Do you play any games?'

31

The word game made Ronald's thoughts blunder. He remembered his host's daughter, the desk.

'Indeed I do!' said Ronald. 'I play at writing my own books' (an excessive discharge of semen causes fatigue, weakness, decrease in activity . . .)

'You write books!'

'Yes,' said Ronald. 'But I love checkers too' (emaciation, dehydration . . .) He glanced at his hands to calm himself.

Carl Bauer's checkers collection occupied the otherwise empty bookshelves at one end of the living room (heat and pains in the membranes of the brain . . .) Checkers from different parts of the world were positioned in ranks as if they might march into the rest of the house, overrun it. A game was in progress at a small table, Ukrainian wood against American rubber. 'These are my men,' Carl Bauer said. 'They're as strong or as weak as their commander. I play twice a day. My loyalties are on both sides. In the end, they often slaughter each other.'

Ronald felt Sally pulling at his sleeve, and she whispered to him, 'Listen to that!' (a loss in the acuity of the senses . . .)

'A most magnificent game,' said Ronald, ignoring the child. 'A masculine game' (*tabes dorsalis*, simplemindedness and various disorders).

'I only play by myself since Dicker beat me in twenty minutes,' Carl Bauer replied.

Then Carl Bauer remembered his manners.

'Call me Carl,' he cried. 'Please. Ronald. And you must have a cocktail! You know, I once wrote a book too, a very long time ago. It was my doctoral dissertation.'

He had all the special equipment, the glasses and phials, the ice in a round plastic container, the olives,

32

the maraschino, the twizzlers: oh, for an American son-in-law! Stanislav hated cocktails, and always demanded red wine.

'I'll have a Bloody Mary, please,' said Ronald, calm and collected now.

Sally dropped away as Ronald headed for the sofa. He noted the prairie design of the covering. The furniture was American pioneer. Patriotic people, thought Ronald. My parents were too rich to enjoy kitsch. Everyone watched as Ronald's trouser backsides sank slowly on to the range. He stretched out his long legs, draped his arms along the sofa back. Connie came and sat down next to him, at a discreet interval.

Carl Bauer's recliner stood on Connie's side. He was about to sit down, frowned at Connie and squeezed into a small, uncomfortable chair on Ronald's side.

'Do you know Palmerston North?' he asked. 'It's a beautiful, historic town. It really deserves to be more than a suburb. Now companies over in Manhattan have plans to build highrises along the river. I think that they are going to be ordinary buildings. Palmerston North needs something special, something important. Not just a bigger movie house on Main Street. And have you seen the Amusement Park? It's an open sore here, it attracts the – '

'Not just a bigger movie house, Mr Bauer, it's time for dinner,' Gerda interrupted. She appraised the situation, Mr Bauer squeezed into that little chair, and grimaced at Connie.

She had cooked her finest German cuisine. Every dish had a bit of animal muscle: sauerbraten, dumplings that lay like little brains, doused with muscle sauce, just as in life, as well as the head of cabbage smothered with bacon. Ronald

33

sat at Carl Bauer's right hand and appeared to listen carefully as Dicker said grace, in a shrill, loud chant. Ronald's face (everyone watched but Dicker) seemed suffused with piety, eyes half closed, nostrils flaring, possibly because of the bacon. 'Thank you, Dicker,' he said afterwards. It was the last time during that meal that he directed his deep but soft voice towards the others. Afterwards, his attention was held by Carl Bauer, who addressed him on the quality of American life, ranging from Buicks to the benefits left by the Pilgrims on the American psyche. Carl Bauer's only objection was to the courts. 'They're useless institutions for the control of right and wrong. Because they threaten rather than persuade. Do you agree? Only the Church can reach chronic offenders, with gentle arguments about obedience. We've come a long way since the extermination of infidels.' Whereupon Ronald succeeded in interrupting: 'Catholici vero qui, crucis assumpto charactere, ad haereticorum exterminium se accinxerint, illa gaudeant indulgentia, illoque sancto privilegio sint muniti, quod accedentibus in Terrae sanctae subsidium conceditur.'

Carl Bauer sat back from the table, leaning his head to one side.

'That was St Thomas Aquinas speaking,' said Ronald.

And Carl Bauer replied, 'Meat in America is something different. It's part of our heritage to eat meat in great quantity here. The average American man, John Doe, is taller and stronger than any other nation's average man. That's because of the meat.' The main course was dismissed. 'I mustn't eat pastry,' Carl Bauer exclaimed as Gerda brought in the apfelstrudel. 'The children shouldn't have a fat grandfather! Oh well.' He took a large helping.

In Gerda's ministry, supper ran its course in a slow,

stately fashion. Inevitably there was nothing more to do but disband. Ronald volunteered to say grace, but Carl Bauer wanted the chance to give a small speech, with a few words of welcome to the special guest. He stood up, a short man of ordinary stature made vast by the intensity of his dark blue eyes.

He looked over everyone's head to say, 'Thanks be to our Lord!' He continued to look up, without saying a word. Slowly, at his sides, his hands contracted into fists. One could see the knuckles turn white from the pressure, and a tremble shook his paunch and his jowls as he said, 'I want to give special thanks to our guest for joining us today.' He wanted to say more, could not think of anything, was frustrated by his inability and then murmured, 'Thanks be to our Lord,' one more time. As if to say 'Amen' to that, the house was suddenly riven by clocks ringing six p.m.

As the party returned to the living room, Gerda forged ahead to remove the cocktail glasses, and in the turbulence she created Sally steered to the stranger's side and nabbed him. 'Come up to my room for a sec, please.'

She studied him, deciding whether she still liked him. In any case, she liked what she saw, including his forehead, which was engraved with a deep but somehow fresh line, like a wrinkle on a newborn. He, for his part, recognized the assault: she was taking him to be her father. He didn't mind this novel request, didn't even trouble to relight the pipe that hung cold between his lips. He accepted his instant paternity to Connie's beautiful blonde child. He begged Carl Bauer to excuse him for a moment, took Sally's sticky hand and allowed himself to be dragged up a flight of stairs, through a corridor, his head bobbing automatically – what politeness will

35

affect! – at the huge crucifix that hung there, and on into the den.

'I have something terrible to tell you,' Sally said.

He smelled children's underwear and plastic dolls, found the odour unfamiliar and repulsive, and hastily relit his pipe. He dragged on it heavily, watched the smoke climb into the air and saw beyond the cloud. He shuddered at the sight of a man's room flooded with camp-beds, toys, children's clothes. He sat down in a leather easy chair. Very comfortable. Sally unpacked her briefcase. She took a black school folder with a white cross in the cover and laid its contents on Carl Bauer's desk.

He leafed through the folder without paying close attention; the clippings had the soft, cheap paper and gaudy colours of the boulevard Press. Then he began to concentrate. 'IS HITLER HIDING IN AMERICA?' read the headlines of the *American Inquirer*. 'MORE PROOF THAT HITLER IS NOT DEAD!' asserted the *Daily Mail*. And on and on: 'ADOLF MOST LIKELY IN THE EASTERN UNITED STATES, an expert warns'. 'SUBURBANITES WARNED TO KEEP A WATCH!' 'DANGER OF NAZI IN OUR MIDST'.

Sally looked at him and whispered, 'Don't you see? It's Opa. Our grandfather. There's no doubt about it. Hiding right here. Downstairs. You've just eaten dinner with him.'

Ronald stood and stared, his expression befuddled, his pipe hanging limply.

'Look, he's from Austria, so was my grandmother. Gerda's German. He won't say why they left. He does hate Jews. He wears that ridiculous moustache. Mommy says old people keep the style they wore during that part of their youth when they were happiest. It all makes sense. You have to help me prove it!' said Sally.

36

She flounced on to her camp-bed, annoyed that he was taking so long to understand.

'But your grandfather is a very pious Catholic,' replied Ronald, words and thoughts running like express trains along divergent tracks, for he suddenly remembered his own title, 'The Effects of Piety on Secrets'. 'Gosh!' he explained. 'Jiminy Cricket! What the heck!'

There was the rest of the parade, his room-mate out in front with the Madonna,

followed by Carl Bauer in an ankle-length black trench coat, shaking his fist, his mouth a huge round hole as he screeched, 'Bless me, Father!'

'He's bad!' Sally repeated.

''Course he's bad. Remember Peter the Apostle, Sally? He denied Jesus three times, and then he became the first pope. The model pope is someone you can't trust for more than six hours.'

She stared.

No use explaining theological problems to an eight year old. 'Leave this to me,' Ronald said. 'You're a very bright, courageous girl indeed. I'm sure your grandfather is a very good man, no matter what he used to be. He could become a cardinal. He's made a lovely home for you. The cuisine is excellent. Real cordon bleu.'

Sally sat up on her camp-bed. 'He should admit it, I think. He always makes us admit every little thing we do wrong. And then he talks about it for weeks afterwards. He acts as if he's never done anything wrong in his life. But when I ask him about his life before Cincinnati, he gets angry. And so does my mom. Really angry. A venial sin. I could make them repeat it hundreds of times a day.'

She opened a drawer of Carl Bauer's desk. 'He doesn't like us going in here, but he won't miss this.' She handed him a photograph. 'He's a good Catholic, all right, but I don't know if he's repented for all of his sins.'

The photograph showed Carl Bauer sitting on a rock in the woods, his granddaughter on his lap. Sally sat in a position of trust on his knees. She was laughing passionately, as children do when they're in love. In the photo, the foliage was the pale green of early spring. 'He used to carry it around in his wallet. He said it was his favourite photo. Since he put it in his desk he never looks at it. You can have it.'

'You seem to trust him here,' Ronald observed.

'That was before we moved in with him. My mother says he's just bitter because our grandmother died. She died over Easter last year. When they buried her at the church cemetery, he insulted the attendants lowering her coffin into the ground. He didn't raise his voice. He spoke real quietly. He mentioned it to them. "You're bastards for bumping the coffin. Go and do that to your dozens of relatives, but not to one of my only." That's what he said. And after that, he became so obsessed with the Jews.'

Ronald looked at the faces on the photograph. 'And your grandmother, was she nice?'

'She was nice, yes,' the child said, in a collected way. 'The initials of her maiden name were E.B., by the way. Eva Braun. I found a monogrammed handkerchief.' She produced an embroidered cloth and he inspected it. 'I don't know why he wouldn't let her go to the hospital when she was feeling badly. He never even let her go to the dentist. She had no more teeth. When we lived in New York, and came here to play in the garden, the neighbour, PJ, always snuck over to see us and asked us what was the matter with our grandmother. "She should go to a doctor, she's not a'tall well." That's how PJ talks. She was always talking to us about "Your dear grandma's fainting spells", PJ was. I never saw her faint. And our grandfather wouldn't let PJ in the door. He said, "She tries to talk us into wasting our time with doctors, well, they're all quacks!" He still says that. He says it's because he doesn't trust anything that originated in the brains of scientists and doctors, seeing what a fool his own son-in-law is, and he's famous. He's a fanatic about mistrusting doctors.'

She looked at him with confidence. 'Can't you do an analysis of his face down at the morgue?'

'An analysis. Well, in a crude way. I'm not a detective, Sally. But let me think about it.' He was still recovering from the surprise: Hitler, Connie's father!

'Has my grandchild been a good host?' Carl asked.

'Yes. She showed me everything. Unfortunately, I have to catch the bus now.'

Patricia June, PJ to her friends, watched Ronald and Connie stroll past from her porch window. She bet Connie was wondering how to treat her boyfriend if he tried to kiss her goodbye in the extreme visibility of a suburban street. It could be awkward to hold him off without hurting his feelings. More likely, Connie dreaded that her date might not try. PJ knew well how it felt to be caught in a crossfire of one's own feelings. Her advice to the boy would be: When the bus comes into view, speak from a distance, 'I'd like to kiss you,' and shake her hand. She probably adores good manners now, learned her lesson on Stanislav.

PJ wondered how Carl was taking it. She had a good idea; she knew Carl well enough. She had played Canasta with him and Eva every single Wednesday evening. Then, when her husband Stratford died, Eva had stopped inviting

her. It was obvious why. 'You're good-looking, gal,' PJ
told herself, 'that's why.' She had argued with herself, 'But
listen, five years older than Eva. She has no call a'tall to be
jealous just because of some *ima'ginary* good looks. Me!
Good-looking! Never. Although my colouring's unusual,
green eyes, black hair. And I'm top-heavy, like Connie.
She suspects me to be the merry widow. Probably because
I'm not even Lutheran any more. She holds that against
me, ten to two.' In fact it was long before Stratford's death
that PJ first noted that the neighbour was attractive. At
first, she only suspected herself of liking him, a suspicion
spoken in the tongue of sweet, singing thoughts about
Carl. During their four-handed Canasta games she banned
any sentimental feelings, as a violation of friendship. But
then no one could have noticed the thoughts besides herself
and so she allowed them to amuse her. Soon she was
spending hours with Carl every day and no one, including
Carl himself, ever suspected. Then Stratford died, and the
necessity of looking out for her future made her ruthless.
At the funeral service, her posture gave her away to Eva,
like a scream.

   – She kept her torso turned to Carl.

   – She had a way of talking more softly to him than to
others.

   And since no one had paid Carl so much attention in
years, he stayed turned to her and his voice returned the
softness.

   Eva drew the conclusion. PJ knew about conclusions
and could figure Eva's out, anyway: she was obsessed
with tidiness, small chance she'd invite untidy feelings
into the house. Make a big mess. Could take years to
clean up. Canasta was cancelled.

   For several months after Stratford's passing away, PJ

had cried every Wednesday evening from seven when Carl should have been mixing her cocktail to nine-thirty when he would have walked her home (he would have insisted, he was a gentleman) after a rousing game of three-handed Canasta. Then one Wednesday afternoon she took action.

She counted her money. It was a fair amount; Stratford had been a dentist. Their son York reckoned he'd buy himself a bigger house. He wanted his mother to move in with his wife and brats in Tucson. PJ would have none of it. She had counted the money, and that same evening she had trotted over to the Bauers', invited or no, and rung the doorbell. Oh what a beautiful afternoon. Happy's youthful bark coming as close to a roar as he'd ever managed. Gerda's eye in the peephole. The door opening fast and wide. 'Oh my poor PJ!' she said. 'Why haven't you come sooner?'

'I wasn't invited.'

'I know. You just go in to the master and mistress. Take a seat. If you ask me.'

PJ couldn't resist giving Gerda a sloppy kiss on her thin grey cheek. She buzzed happily, and pushed PJ through the hallway to the living room. PJ refused to cross the threshold. The Bauers looked up from their Gin Rummy. Eva said, 'Why my goodness, dear, come in.' PJ stayed where she was. She had some pride. She blurted her invitation from the doorway like a Western Union messenger: a free trip to visit the De Ville ancestral home in Strasbourg, Alsatia: 'That's in France.' On one condition. They travel together.

She had prepared the itinerary: first-class ship to Southampton, 'then per train to Alsatia. Where all my grandparents were born. Then per rental car south, to Monte Carlo, where we'll play Canasta for chips.'

41

Since Eva's death, the trip was PJ's favourite memory. She tuned in to it several times a day, more often than to any soap operas or any memory of her honeymoon. The trip had been glorious, full of promise. Now that Eva was no longer there, she had a chance to make good the promise. PJ saw Carl's problems (Connie moving in; Connie finding a new man) with the personal interest of an involved party.

She was going to give him some time to mourn. A long time, for the sake of discretion, would make the middle of December. The season to be jolly. Then she'd drop by casually, on a Wednesday. The day the children had their long day at school, something extracurricular – it was some coincidence! – so they wouldn't be there to interfere. Fate had obviously laid its plans carefully. In this case, for her success.

PJ saw Connie return from her walk, and the door fall shut behind her. 'December, here I come!' she gloated.

3

Huge Dr Miele had a malpractice death on his porcelain table. He lit up a fresh cigar, sat down, adjusted his rubber apron, and addressed Dr Hake over his shoulder. 'Say Donalronal, what was that poem you invented for your publication? About organ colours? Very sentimental, but otherwise clever.'

Dr Hake had a body-parts-in-the-drain case. No prayer of sitting down. He stooped over the autopsy table, the parts laid out in a row. Miele was a lucky bastard, sitting like that. He recited:

> 'The body's closed.
> Inside it glows,
> Darkness tends each gorgeous tone
> The corporal gardens always bloom.
> Darkness loves Vermilion,
> Lily, Lapus, Rose Bengal,
> Blindly, darkness loves them all.

> The body's beauty comes to light
> When death,
> Visiting, lets us in:
> Splendid sight.'

'Exactly!' said Dr Miele and made his incision.

43

Dr Hake arranged the body parts, while in his mind he toiled over the riddle of Carl Bauer. He was measuring bones to establish the size and sex of the victim. Left femur, 426.2 mm. The Church had scored a great coup recruiting Adolf Hitler into the flock. His Most Benign Last Word had not chosen to have him caught and humiliated by execution, but had turned him over to ritual and organized superstition. Left tibia, 345 mm. Dr Hake had heard of death-bed confessions of the most heinous crimes for which the evil-doer had never paid one penny of his debt to society, patella 397 long; 40.0 wide, on the contrary, he had died happy, surrounded by persons who loved and respected him, and who could recount only tales of his goodness, and – this was the common denominator that had caught Dr Hake's attention – piety. Sternum length with proc. ensiform, 185 mm. All had been in the hands of the Church. All had presumably confessed their crimes to a priest, Bless me, Father, just because I have sinned. Without proc. ensiform 141.0 mm. I have killed. You'll have to talk to the bishop about that one. But it was during a Just War! Well, in that case: how often, my child? Once, ten times, I have tormented and raped. In the name of the Father, the Son, humerus 272. Looks like a female. I absolve you of your guilt. Scapula 147 wide, 160 long. In truth, Hake had never ever heard of such death-bed confessions, but guessed that they happened all the time. Wasn't it preposterous to believe that The Magnificent Scale tipped in favour of those who did the most disgusting deeds, and then, upon expressing regret, were encouraged to forget the whole thing? Radius 223, clavicle 136 mm. A female, definitely. No doubt washed down the drain by the ludicrous, ineffectual male of the species. Females were too practical; they knew how hard it was to find a cheap plumber.

Dr Hake took the plastic bag with the puzzle of the pelvis and emptied it on the table. Piety obscured secrets (here was the pubic bone) rather than unlocked them (the fossa acetabuli), merged with secrets (symphysi), became secrets themselves. (A pelvis told you everything.) The ritual and metaphors of belief undermined rather than supported genuine piety. Metaphor as illness. That's another book, Dr Hake admonished. One at a time.

Dr Hake jotted down the sums on a pad as he went, and soon had the size of the corpse worked out, four foot ten, plus the head. That was still missing. Then he began laying the parts out like a puzzle. He imagined Hitler going to his first confession.

Dark and muggy in the confessional. It's been in use all day long. The screen slides open and the priest whispers, 'Proceed, please.' He has a mid-West accent.

'Bless me, Father, for I have sinned. My last confession was – forty years ago.'

Shuffling of robes. The voice comes from very close. 'When was the last time you attended mass?!'

'Also forty years ago, Father.'

Silence. Adolf Hitler hears footsteps outside the confessional. He watches the curtain wafting gently, as someone passes by. Finally the priest says, 'Can you remember how to make your confession?'

'Yes, Father.'

'Then proceed, please.'

'I will start with the big sins, Father.' He hesitates, summoning his will. 'I have been impure, Father.'

The priest sighs. Then his voice comes, monotonous and sad. 'In thought, word or deed, my son.'

'In thought, word and deed.'

The priest picks up speed, this is rote. 'By yourself, or with others?'

'By myself and with others.'

'Male or female?'

'Female.'

'Relations?'

'Yes.'

'Which relations?'

'My cousin, once removed.'

'And how often?'

'Repeatedly.'

'Can you say how often?'

'Too often to say.' At this point, Hitler's voice breaks with emotion.

'I can hear the sorrow in your voice,' comments the priest, still bored. 'Do you think that you will be able to abstain from sinning the mortal sin of impurity? Are you strong enough? You are aware that if you die with this sin on your soul you will go to hell – '

'I am, Father.'

'Proceed, then.'

'I have to think, Father. I was in the war, so indirectly I was involved in killing.'

'Did you kill anyone yourself?'

'I did not.'

The priest sighs, and waits for more.

'I did not believe in Christ. I said so.'

'Do you believe now?'

'Yes. And I was angry. Very often. I was gluttonous.'

'Are there foods you cannot resist?' asks the priest with new interest.

'Pastry,' says Adolf Hitler. 'I cannot resist pastry.'

'Hmm,' says the priest.

Hitler is silent.

'Anything more?'

'I don't think so.'

The priest reflects for a long time. 'Since this is your very first confession in a long time, it is clear to me that your greatest weakness is weakness of the flesh. You must learn to control yourself. And as a real proof to our Lord that you mean it seriously, I give you as your penitence the duty to say one rosary. And, in addition, to prove to yourself your own resolve, you should abstain from eating pastry for one entire month.'

They pray the Act of Contrition together.

Hitler leaves the confessional as Carl Bauer. He kneels at the altar railing and looks at Jesus. He imagines that his soul is white. The angels are figure-skating on the surface. And he prays. 'Thank you, Almighty Force of Life!'

'What you daydreaming about, Sunny Jim?' called Dr Miele out of a cloud of cigar smoke. 'Your pipe's gone out. Must be girls again. I'm finished. The surgeon who operated on this poor slob here is going to have an unpleasant week.' He untied his apron, squinted over at Dr Hake's corpse and said, 'Looks like a twenty-six-year-old female to me. She'll be about five foot four when they find the head, as tall as my wife.'

Dr Hake ignored him. He was deep in his speculations.

But what proof does the Church have that Hitler has really repented?

In the olden days the sinner heaped ashes on his head. He tore his best clothing, gave all of his money to the next priest, and one had proof of his atonement. Nowadays, the Church only collected exorbitant tuition fees at their prep schools.

Perhaps, Dr Hake ventured, one should try to apply medical methodology to the problem of Carl Bauer's secret. Regard it as disease. His condition was obviously not critical. In fact, the patient might be entirely recovered, and his illness have purely historical value.

Standing over the corpse, Dr Hake wiped his forehead, which was spattered by the end of the ecological chain which began with hope, led to anxiety, and ended in sweat. An ambition articulated for the first time often causes a lot of damage to bystanders because it over-stimulates the hope function of the brain. Not exactly Freude schöner Götterfunken. Something much stronger.

Dr Hake began to compose in his best medical prose:

A seventy-one-year-old man from Germany was living in a NY suburb with his family. Although he showed healthy patriotism and collected Americana, he felt anti-Semitic and complained that politics left a bitter taste in his mouth. He had attended church regularly but had failed to lose his hatred of the Jewish race. He claimed that this was an essential part of Church dogma. He did not smoke or drink, but enjoyed pastry despite a slight weight problem. He responded well to weak creatures, an old dachshund, and to nature, but had a poor tolerance of children and untidiness. His consumption of meat was based on the belief that it made Americans strong. He was prone to excreting monologues over dinner.

Screening tests results:

Obedience as a higher value: Strong positive
Fascination with military: Weak positive (chess)
Politically active: Negative
Interest in history: Negative

Racial consciousness: Positive
Fetish for ritual and regalia: Positive
Blaming the liberal establishment for society's woes:
Strong positive
Delusions of grandeur: Negative.

Differential diagnosis:

– Conservative, traditional Catholic
– Nazi ideologue.

Suggested therapy:

Until a definite diagnosis has been made, none required
for the patient, but the people with whom he comes
into contact must be protected from exposure. The best
protection is education.

Dr Hake regarded his tiny, barbed script aligned along
the white sheet. Beautiful. All he needed was a simple
admission that Carl Bauer was Hitler, a 'how'd you guess',
and he would know that his style of analysis worked
much more reliably than any half-hearted, self-deceiving
confession.

He remembered he hadn't seen Connie all day. At once,
he concentrated on his corpse, solving the puzzle in record
minutes. Barry, the court photographer, came and took
photos. He found Dr Hake flushed and so attractive that
he made a couple of shots of him too, for his own
archives.

Since the sudden advent of their passion, Drs Bauer and
Hake had found no place to meet in private for a little
baseball. Dr Guttenberg was deeply suspicious, and had
alerted Dr Miele that something could be afoot between

49

them. 'And I don't mean just concerning feet either,' said Dr Guttenberg. Dr Miele did not care what others were doing with one another. Behind his back, he began calling his colleague 'Dr Gutterberg'. His nicknames were his private pleasure. Not caring about others made him discreet. He was happily married himself and could no longer imagine any reason why two people could be interested in each other. When he saw ads with couples on them, he refused to buy the product. So he wasn't going to keep an eye on anyone. 'Nodda cians,' he said.

To which Dr Guttenberg replied, 'Well, I just hope they know about professional conduct, and all that.'

It was understood by all that romance on the job was strictly inappropriate, unprofessional and made others envious. The couple's only recourse was to keep their friendship under several wraps of casual acquaintance. Here Connie's evasiveness stood her in good stead. In public she treated Dr Hake in a friendly, indifferent manner. Whereas Dr Hake could not keep the heat from his cheeks, and always stood several inches too close to her Attributes. Dr Guttenberg, observing this, decided that, 'Hake has a bad case of being in love. The poor waspie bastard. I'm not giving him any lessons. Maybe she drinks coffee with him, and he thinks it's encouragement. Dr Bauer's not interested. I can tell that in a woman.' And he relaxed his vigilance a little, and allowed his contempt to show.

This gave the two a bit more licence. One day when Dr Bauer and Dr Hake bumped into each other on their way to a new case Dr Hake asked her politely, 'Have you ever been down in the tunnels?'

Dr Hake replaced his pipe in its etui, always a sign that he was up to no good, and they set off. The stairs led directly down to the City undertaking school's 'Practical

Year' office. From there a network of dark, hot corridors connected the morgue to the mental ward and to the main building. The hospital machinery was kept down there, but wild cats, rats and hobos also took refuge in the storage nooks. Occasionally a green-clad orderly strode by, or the cats would erupt in a wild rumble. The doctors never used the tunnels. Drs Bauer and Hake made a handsome lab-coated couple. When they reached a bum sleeping in a sodden obstruction across their path, Dr Hake gallantly swept her into his arms, and carried her over. During this manoeuvre she dared to slip a kiss on his neck.

Crossing the next such bum, Dr Hake slowed down and half-way over, straddling the snoring man, they explored first base until they began to lose the sensation of solid ground beneath their feet.

Just in time, an orderly pushing a corpse called out, 'Scuse us.' Dr Hake recovered his composure. He put Dr Bauer down on the other side of the hurdle, and as they continued their stroll he began a lengthy discourse on his latest bone-reconstruction case. Suddenly he switched the subject altogether.

'Tell me about your father,' he said. 'Where was he born?'

She missed a step, almost stumbling. He caught her arm, and held her. Worry bruised her features. He touched her cheek to encourage her, watching his white fingertips as they brushed her equally fair skin.

She seemed to relax. 'What strange questions you ask! He was born in a small town in Austria,' she said, 'But we came to the United States when I was a child. We moved to Cincinnati.'

'Before the war?'

'Yes. Before, of course. We saw the war coming.'

51

'You don't like to talk about it.'

'I don't like to be thought of as a foreigner, that's all,' she said. 'And I've never asked you where you were born, have I? I don't think it's important.'

'I was born in Greenwich, Connecticut,' Dr Hake volunteered. 'My father was a businessman. He owned a chain of funeral homes. From there, you usually go into city politics, but he didn't. He was not very intelligent. No one was very intelligent in the family. They were all interested in money. But they're deceased. Massive aneurysms à deux after eating too much fondue. During Valsalva Manoeuvre. The house had four bathrooms.'

'So you were well off.'

'Filthy rich, my dear. I was expected to take over the business. But it didn't interest me. My sister is doing very well with it. She's diversified into cosmetics. I'm more interested in acquiring knowledge than money. Knowledge is my great love. I want to accumulate it. I'm absolutely greedy to know you better, and see what your heart says.'

'My heart must be like an open book to you,' she replied.

'With half the pages stuck together.'

'And a quarter of the pages torn out,' she finished.

After this remark they stopped worrying about the orderlies, the bums or the cats. Down in the tunnels it was warm, dark, and damp as a tropical beach at night. The couple must be left in peace for a while, in a niche, bedded down on Dr Hake's white lab coat, a little blood on the front, nothing ugly, and very comfortable. It is no one's business now; they are asking themselves questions of a private and not a pious nature. Faintly at first, they still register the hope that their unexplained, unprofessional absence together will not be noticed by Dr Gutterberg. Very soon, the term absence loses its meaning in the extraordinary force of the present.

Sister Mary Angela's class was clicking along at full intellectual tempo.

'Where do the little children who are not baptized go? Jerry?'

'To limbo.'

'Why?'

'Because they never had the chance to decide.'

'Right! They never learned about the available choices. Grown-ups have the choice. Those who turn their backs on the Church go to hell.

'Children. You can instruct people about God. Even little children can teach grown-ups a thing or two. At your age, you have the most remarkable powers of persuasion. Because of your innocence.'

The eyes of the children glittered with lust to convert a grown-up.

'Adults who've turned their backs on the Church can be brought back into the fold before they die and go to hell.'

'What about a Jew?' asked Dicker.

Sister Mary Angela sighed. 'A grown-up Jew?' She hesitated. 'That's a very great problem,' she said. 'With the Jews. Let us pray.'

'Daddy is exempted,' Sally said later. 'I know it. He always ate fish with us on Fridays.'

'But I bet he doesn't any more,' Dicker said.

'Yes, he does too,' Sally said. 'He says it's healthy, once a week fish.'

'Shouldn't we pray for him anyway?' asked Dicker.

Dicker prayed ferociously. He set himself a goal of one entire rosary at bedtime to save his father. Later, he began to worry that it might not be enough. Two rosaries would be better, but three would really play it safe. He always fell asleep before finishing his quota. He began to go into debt to God. He kept an IOU. Within a week he owed dozens of rosaries, with no end in sight, and he slept heavily in order to escape the suffocating knowledge of his debts piling up.

A few mornings later, Dr Guttenberg looked out of his office window and noted an elderly male Caucasian walking along the alleyway that led to the morgue. He carried a plaid carrier bag and walked with the uncertain, absent-minded gait Dr Guttenberg felt was typical of the bereaved. When the old man started up the morgue front steps, Dr Guttenberg hurried to get Alice, who, being fatter and more resolute than delicate Blessed, generally acted as the bouncer in such situations.

'Alice is powdering her nose, darling,' said Blessed.

The unidentified visitor was Carl Bauer. As soon as he entered the front hall, the contents of his little plaid bag began to yodel and thrash about. Dr Guttenberg returned to the hall and Carl Bauer addressed him. 'I want to see my daughter.'

'I'm sorry, you'll have to follow the usual procedure, you can't just come here,' Dr Guttenberg said. He took his arm and turned him towards the door.

'But I want to see my daughter!' Carl protested.

Then Dr Guttenberg recognized the German accent.

Connie was horrified to see her father. 'How on earth did you get here!' she said.

'I drove of course, like any human being. I drove

carefully. I never skidded once on all those turns on Riverside Drive, I braked gracefully. Driving is an old pleasure of mine.' He addressed the general public now. 'The new highway running along the river will be a great joy for the motorist.'

Meanwhile Blessed had secured Alice, pursued by Dr Miele, and after that came Dr Hake, followed closely by two technicians. They stood in the front hall and Carl Bauer addressed them all.

'It's funny that I haven't driven distances for years. I'll start again now. I've thought of driving my Buick across America.'

'Papa, calm down, that's a long way.'

'Well, Dr Hake here can accompany me. It smells funny in here, Connie. You haven't left something out of the refrigerator?'

'Come to the office, Papa. That smells all right.'

He came, the others following; everyone squeezed into the secretaries' office and watched as the old man took a seat. He accepted Alice's cookies, then he opened the plaid bag and allowed Happy, trembling, his nose writhing, to emerge. As soon as the dog had calmed down, he was delivered unto Alice's spacious lap. Alice came right out and said it. 'You're from Germany, aren't you. I know it. I just adore your accent.'

'Yes,' he said. 'I'm from Germany. Austria, actually.' He looked at all the tall standing men in white coats, liked what he saw, ignored the women, and sighed. 'Oh, I could tell you more about America than about Germany, though, about how I first saw this country and I thought – America!

'America,' he said. 'When we arrived in America we knew no one would be there waiting for us. No one waving to us. Just America. For six days, we saw nothing but ocean. Then, the morning of the seventh day was clear and bright, and soon there appeared a faint line of something hidden by the distance. After several hours this took on substance, stretching to meet us, then spreading to greet us; then it surrounded us: America.'

'The way Mr Bauer says America,' marvelled Alice.

'When I came up from Jamaica,' said Blessed, 'all I thought about was this toothache I had.'

Carl Bauer's face and posture changed as he talked; intensity straightened his back, and smoothed his face. He continued, speaking easily, but rapidly.

'On deck next to us the other passengers were crying like children.'

'Maybe they had toothaches too,' said Blessed.

'I remember one man in a black velvet hat. He kept pointing to the shore with its small houses like pebbles. He shouted, "There's Bronx! That's where we're going to live, Bronx!" His hat fell backwards off his head. A small round woman behind him grabbed it and swatted him with it. "Bronx won't like you if your hat's all dirty."

'My wife Eva was standing behind them, she was disgusted. "What's the use of sentimentality!" she said to me. She had a map of New York with her, which she unfolded and stuck under the little man's nose. "Look," she told him. "That's not the Bronx you're pointing to. That's Brooklyn." My wife's first emotion on arriving in America was contempt. Oh, but not mine!'

'And mine neither,' said Alice. 'Blessed, you're silly-ungrateful.'

'Listen here, I had a toothache and I had to wait in line for five hours to get through some inspection. Didn't you have no inspection, Mr Bauer?'

56

'Yes, we did. Before we were allowed to disembark. It's true. I remember our suitcases lying open in front of us.' He gestured to an imaginary trunk. 'The official poking around the sides.' Carl Bauer poked. Then he swept his hand and said, 'Finally he slammed the cases shut and they slid off the counter in the direction of the landing. I stood all alone on the top stair. There was a big crowd below. The gulls screeched at me. Then I went down. And I became part of America then.'

'Anyone for another cookie?'

'I'm talking too much. It's just – I am romantic about America. In love stories, the first time one looks and thinks, "This is it! This moment counts for years, no matter what happens afterwards." For me, America will always look and smell and feel a little the way it did on my arrival.' His voice had become hoarse.

'The boat on due course in the radiant river, passing along the jammed isles in a sudden shower of mist, the blessing of the Statue, the gradual approach after the preparation, while the gulls cheered and the ropes whistled and then the resolute ringing of the ramps let out on the landing.'

Here he stopped, and his energy drained visibly from him; he became elderly, frail, and finally unhappiness took back the upper hand over memory. 'This is the first time I've ever visited you, Connie. Now I have to go home.'

He stood up with difficulty, fumbled for the dog, and had to be helped out of the room by Dr Hake, who watched his own hand as it cupped Hitler's elbow.

Gerda picked the children up from school.

'Betty told me girls bleed,' said Dicker.

'Boys bleed too,' said Sally.

57

'They don't.'

'They do.'

Gerda said she didn't know about it, since she was never married. In the evening, the children appealed to Connie.

'Betty told me that boys put their dingalings inside the girls' creases,' said Sally. 'See? She tells a lot of weird stories, Dicker. You're a fool to believe her. A dope.'

'Her mother told her so,' said Dicker.

Connie spoke. 'Betty's mother is not a doctor. She hasn't much of a clue about medical problems. So don't listen to her.'

Upstairs in their room, Sally said, 'Betty uses the word peni all the time. Even though it's a mortal sin to use the word peni. Impurity of word.'

She was satisfied, and turned away to think about other things.

All evening the word buzzed around Dicker's head, peni peni peni. He prayed, 'Please God, don't let me be impure in thought,' but the word found no escape from his mind. Sighing, he fetched a pad, which he kept next to his comic book, and then he started to keep a tally, to keep track, so that when the priest asked him, 'How often, my child?' he could give a precise answer.

4

Did Carl Bauer ever dream? 'I never dream,' he told his granddaughter once, when she complained about falling off a cliff in a nightmare. 'If you didn't want to dream, you wouldn't. You probably want to dream.'

'You have a bad conscience, that's why you dream,' said Gerda. 'Opa always has a clear conscience. I dream sometimes, too. About forgetting a chore. But your grandfather, he has a very regular, quiet sleep. And when he wakes up in the morning, he knows what he has to do.'

When Carl Bauer woke up, he looked at the time according to a pendulum clock on the wall opposite his bed. He washed, and dressed in the clothes Gerda had laid out for him. He knelt down at a prayer stool facing the corner, and prayed with intensity, as Gerda, who sometimes peeked, could tell you, until the clocks chimed nine, and then he stayed downstairs until they struck seven. Two (2) times a day, at ten and at three, he continued an ongoing game of checkers for exactly one half ($\frac{1}{2}$) hour. Three (3) times a day he took Happy for a walk, and returned ten (10) minutes before he washed his hands and used the toilet, finishing ten (10) minutes before he sat down at the dining-room table. He did everything according to the clocks. 'How-often interests him much more than how-much,' Gerda liked to report, as if it was great wisdom. After mass, when the other church-goers asked, out of politeness, how the family was, she described the minutiae of Mr Bauer's schedule. She did not notice when they yawned or looked over her head to see if any friends were passing by. She could not imagine that this information could bore anyone. When she spelled it all out to Connie and the children she concluded, 'How-often is much more important than how-much, which is probably what interests Stanislav.'

Carl appreciated Gerda's interest in his schedule, and although he didn't take her seriously as a conversationalist he sometimes spontaneously talked to her about this matter. 'How often seems to me of more universal interest, the real significance of greed and generosity, boredom or hard work, the domain of the clock as opposed to the scales. (Not to mention that the scales of justice often tip in ways called ludicrous after the clock has ticked its more lasting judgement.)' At 1207 River Avenue, the clocks were kept as honour guards, their hands extended in permanent salute. Carl Bauer looked at a wall and they hailed him.

Carl Bauer rarely left their company. Once a week he attended mass with the rest of the family. Eva had always lingered in the entrance afterwards to chat with others, while he stood quietly next to her. Since her death he always left the church immediately, snapped at Gerda to hurry, although there was nothing to hurry for. Connie, who was considered a hellraiser by the congregation because she never said hello to anyone, was already out in front on some pretext about fetching the car. In other words, his trip to the morgue had signified plenty – the opening of the cell door, the return to life through the acceptance of Connie's profession, his emancipation from his schedule. But the exhaustion that set in afterwards lasted for days. Even the thought of taking a drive tired him. Tick-tick-tick went the clocks, the sound of a constant parade. One afternoon he decided, if he was too tired to drive his Buick across America, he might at least walk across the driveway and visit his neighbour, PJ.

No sooner had this crossed his mind than Eva's candle reached the end of its wick and flickered out, before the next one was lit, for the first time in nineteen months. Gerda's fault. Gerda was out shopping. The children scattered without a sound. Carl Bauer took a long time finding where she kept the candles. He emptied the contents of the laundry cupboards and the odds-and-ends bin on to the floor, flung them down and left everything lying there. Finally he thought of looking in the closet where Gerda stored extra lightbulbs. Then he had to look for the special matches she used. 'I won't use kitchen matches on Eva's candle,' she repeated every time she lit one. He found the silver matchbox next to the prayer books on a shelf near the television. It took him another ten minutes to light the candle. Having a servant makes one forget how to execute the simplest chores, he grumbled, makes one feeble, 'Not fit for life,' he said out loud. By the time he finished, he wanted to tell someone how unbelievable it was, Gerda's besmirching the candle.

He couldn't find the grandchildren. He went looking. They were not in the yard, not in their room. Then he heard footsteps in the attic. He listened. Giggling. A gasp. Then a long silence. Although it was strictly a violation of his schedule, Carl Bauer clambered up to the storage room under the roof and found them up there on their hands and knees in front of an old laundry hamper. They were gaping at a book.

61

At a glance he recognized the photo of a huge pile of bones. It was despicable filth about concentration camps. Eva had bought that years ago, a cheap paperback, and he had banned it at once. He assumed she had thrown it in the garbage where it belonged. Now he saw that she had merely hidden it in a place only the maid frequented.

'What are you doing?' he asked, although he could see. And then he became silent with disapproval. They cowered on their hands and knees, the book closed on the cold wooden floor in front of them. After a while he said, 'You have disappointed me. My own grandchildren, having prurient interests.'

His anger always deepened and darkened with each minute he could pour over an offence, and there was no predicting exactly when and where his fury would finally spend itself. So, each child holding on to the book, sharing the blame, they handed it over to him, and bolted downstairs. Afraid he would follow them, they pulled on their coats and ran outside. There they played with the leaves that swirled with the wind through the back yard.

Carl Bauer was left behind in the quiet attic. The dust stirred up by intruders drizzled silently around him. He stared at the book in his hands. Then he saw the straw laundry hamper was full of books. He plucked one volume out, and hurled it back in. About Nazi Germany. First came the title, then the rest of the doody. Eva must have collected this on the sly. The hamper revolted him, like a broken toilet. It was heavy. He strained to pick it up, managed to clutch it against his belly and totter downstairs like that. He kept going, past the Bill of Rights, outside into the back yard. The children were chasing leaves, stomping them, trampling and obliterating what was so weak that it could no longer stay in its proper place. Then they saw their grandfather approach without his coat. They backed off, crouched under the rhododendron and watched him deposit the hamper in the middle of the lawn. He had the silver matchbox in his hand. Standing there in his shirtsleeves, the leaves swirling merrily around his legs, he attempted to light a match. The wind blew it out. He lit another. Same fate.

'Dear God!' he mumbled. 'Make the wind stop!' The wind stopped.

He managed to keep the match lit long enough to drop a living flame into the laundry hamper. He peered down and watched the effect. The wind picked up again, encouraged the fire that was eating its way through the old pages.

The neighbours' faces appeared in their windows. Well, it was his lawn. He could burn a laundry hamper if he wanted. It was his money. And there's not much of it either, thought PJ, who had some evidence on the matter. Isn't he passionate about things!

The children left the rhododendron. They cavorted, picked up armfuls of leaves and, approaching their grand-father cautiously, dumped them into the laundry basket. He did not reprimand them. The fire fed and grew. They danced around it, increasing their speed as the straw caught fire. He stood watching his torch to Eva, staring at the flames until the fire burned out on its own, and all that remained was a small pile of charcoal. Then he rubbed his arms and shivered.

The children stopped and stared at him. He smiled at them, and winked.

They watched him return slowly into the house. They played in the rhododendron. When Gerda returned, pul-ling a grocery trolley, they did not warn her about the candle, or the treasure she must have known about in the attic, or about Opa winking. When Connie came home she probably walked into the same ambush. Gerda called the children in for supper. Carl Bauer had retired to his room early and didn't want to see anyone that evening. The maid was hoarse, her eyes red and swollen. Connie presided at the dinner table, in a cheerful, sloppy manner. No one raised the subject again, and by the next morning Carl Bauer seemed to have forgotten it entirely.

But after this episode, Carl Bauer began to suffer night-mares himself. For three nights running, he woke up with the weird impression of an object round as a halo fluttering around above his bed. Half asleep, he put his hand over it. It was not a halo, it was cold and hard. At first he had a vision of a gold badge, with an eagle on it. This filled him, for no reason, with such anxiety that he awoke sufficiently to consider the object as a neutral puzzle again. Round and hard. Money, he guessed. A huge, repulsive coin. Then he became lucid with disgust, and the object became clear to him. It was the Nobel Prize.

For three nights running, Carl Bauer turned on his reading lights and left the double bed he shared with a life-size portrait of Eva's head, which stood propped up on her pillow. He grabbed his robe and tottered downstairs from the sleeping quarters on the second floor to his plastic recliner in the living room. He pressed it Down and lay there in darkness, his fist waving in the darkness along the hated circumference of the Nobel Prize. It was an honour, it was society's love. All going to Stanislav.

Gerda zigzagged after him in her arthritic gait, her legs tangling in the flannel nightie she always wore, her long grey hair loose to her waist. She cried, 'Are you ill!'

Three nights, he had given the same reply: 'Ill with worry.' Both lisped without their dentures.

Three nights, she stood at his feet, watching his fist move around, and worried with him until he pressed the recliner button Up again. Then, together, they sighed once and Carl Bauer arose, and together they trudged up the stairs again (Carl Bauer in front of the servant) and returned to their respective beds. During the day Carl Bauer looked drawn and rather fragile.

'My father's not well. He can't seem to sleep,' Connie told Ronald at work, noting that Ronald looked poorly himself.

On the fourth night, Carl Bauer became ill. His heart fluttered hysterically, as do birds who suddenly realize they are trapped in a cage. He made it downstairs, and when Gerda reached him he was lying on the recliner, all the way Down, his hand stiff up in the air like a broken wing. His eyes were closed, his mouth open. She ran a finger around inside his mouth to make sure his dentures were out, and called an ambulance.

PJ's bedroom looked out to the Bauers' bedroom. Since her husband died, she left the shades open, and the light in Carl's room shone into hers. She didn't keep clocks anywhere near her: she had declared her independence of time and the calendar when Stratford died. Instead, she oriented herself according to the lights burning in Carl's room. When his reading lamp went off at night, she switched hers off. When the lamp went on, she turned hers on. So she was aware that he was not sleeping well. On this particular night his bedside lamp remained turned on for several hours, and PJ watched the ambulance arrive, and, a little while later, Carl being loaded

65

into it per stretcher. Connie climbed in the back with him.

PJ reached for the phone and called the operator to ask the time. Two-seven. Exactly as she had feared. The number was significant. Six years earlier, at two-seven on the boat leaving America for Europe, Carl had sat in the cocktail lounge of the ship and said that he deeply regretted leaving America, his homeland. Eva had scolded him: he should be grateful to have any kind of holiday. When she noticed that PJ was listening in, she had switched to German, babbling something, and watching PJ out of the corner of her eye. Carl Bauer had cut her short. 'Spieck Inggg-lisch!' He had looked angrily at PJ and said, 'Forcing me to leave my Hohmländ.'

PJ remembered his words and thought, Two-seven must be my bad-luck number.

The fourth night of Carl Bauer's insomnia, Ronald suffered quite a bout of insomnia himself. At college he had been a nocturnal creature. He had considered the ability to stay up all night a kind of prowess. The less sleep he needed, the more of a man he felt. But with increasing age he began to consider sleep a luxury he deserved, along with an appropriate salary. He liked to retire punctually and with a particular style – he always drank one shot of brandy after putting on his striped silk pyjamas. Sometimes he drank while watching himself in the bathroom mirror. He liked to see himself with slightly bloodshot eyes, the glass to his lips, and then the movement of the prominent Adam's apple that resided just above the maroon and black silk collar. After his last swallow he bared his teeth once, watched his hands putting the glass down on the sink, and headed

66

for bed, where he slept, so he liked to think, power-fully.

But in the middle of the night, his sleep spluttered weak, incontinent as an old man's. Thoughts about Carl Bauer poked at him and he couldn't avoid their insistent fingers. Finally he got up out of his pleasant bed again, dressed with uncharacteristic haste, and took to the unlit streets of his neighbourhood just as Carl Bauer woke up, caught in the headlights of the ambulance, and realized he was tied down. He bellowed; his voice carried several blocks; bedside lights turned on in quick response: 'Goddam' bastards! Let me out of here! Help! Police!'

Ronald reached the morgue while the ambulance was turning on to the dimly lit main road of Palmerston North, and the driver made his decision not to turn on the sirens, because there were no cars on the road, just his windshield wipers; it began to pour. The orderly was a bit puzzled by Connie's bedside manner. She held the patient's hand and spoke very loudly because the rain was drumming on the car roof. 'Papa, this is the most wonderful ride, you would enjoy it, I know.' Her father making no reply. Ronald climbing up the stairs. 'The traffic is parting for us, we are the most important car on the road. We are Moses passing through the Red Sea, we are the President on the way to his inauguration, if only you could see how important and powerful you are!' Meanwhile, Ronald locked himself into his office, looked out of his window and saw that he had miraculously traversed a fair storm without getting wet.

While Carl Bauer's condition was being stabilized, while he was being intubated, hooked up, attached, strapped and flooded with drugs, Dr Hake spent the night at his desk with the patient's photo, as well as several history atlases, with colour illustrations. His research had been eclectic.

As a medical man he had a special contempt for research in the humanities. He considered it unnecessary. He'd combed the Paperback Bookstore on the corner of his block and found lots of material. What he didn't find there he trusted coincidence would throw on his path. In the Great Director's offices, coincidence was one door down from divine intervention, and the clerks went in and out.

Dr Hake stacked his books neatly and went to work, after reprimanding himself that it should take an industrious Princeton buck this long to get to the task which an eight year old had suggested.

But at last, on the night in which Carl Bauer became ill, Dr Hake began the preliminary legwork necessary for a diagnosis. He had a number of pictures of Adolf in various poses, situations and moods: Adolf whipping up a crowd, Adolf grinning at a youngster, Adolf smiling at handsome farmers in shorts, Adolf officially posing for the artist, like a man looking at his reflection in the barber-shop mirror, with an earnest vanity.

Dr Hake picked up his pen and watched his script adorn a sheet of New York City Morgue stationery:

Description of the Patient, Adolf Hitler:

Caucasian male with eye colour: blue; hair colour: black; no distinguishing marks. Face shape: oval; the nose: long, and quite wide at the base, depressed at the root, the mouth small and thin-lipped; the ears: unattached lobes.

His body build: typical endomorph, with sloping shoulders, a wide pelvis, and a tendency to obesity. Non-smoker. No alcohol abuse. Vegetarian.

Because of his stature and his nervous disposition,

the patient is a candidate for nervous colon, hyper-
tension, and cardio-vascular disease. The suspicion of
epilepsy and Parkinson's seems unfounded. The episodes
of tremor reported in his hands and right leg have
been attributed, along with personality changes, to the
patient's abuse of a preparation with brand name 'Dr
Koester's Anti-gas Pills' (Extr. Nux Vom, etr. Bellad,
a,a,o,5; extr. Gent). In view of the current health of the
patient, now called Carl Bauer, it is quite impossible
that he had Parkinson's.

Dr Hake put down his pen and heard the wind railing
against the window-pane. The sign reading 'Mortuary'
swung back and forth. The anti-gas pills had been served to
Hitler by a quack. They had made him drug-dependent and
ill. Perhaps this explains Carl Bauer's hatred of doctors.
Dr Hake reflected on Hitler's personality and regretted his
lack of training in psychology. He picked up his pen and
continued on page two:

Even before his drug-dependency began, the patient was
reported to have suffered bouts of bad temper (something that this observer feels worsens with age). There
is no confirmation of a sadistic streak, or special interest
in the suffering of others. Recorded chronic reliance on
horoscopy, at levels commonly seen in housewives.
High level of self-confidence, to the point of delusion.
On the other hand, he is sociable, articulate, fond
of children and dogs, and idealistic, all traits which
put him in a lower risk-group for psychosomatic and
stress-related disease.
    The stress of office (tension, irregular sleeping habits,
little exercise) obviously took a toll on the patient: the
tremors, the hoarseness caused by cysts on his vocal

chords, as well as the attacks of hysteria were only reported after his life-style changed on account of the war. With proper rest, the patient would have been expected to improve.

Dr Hake laid the photo of Carl Bauer on the table. It showed him in a sitting position, a grey mass among the pastels of springtime, his face shown frontally, slightly from above. His left ear was visible, his left hand, holding on to the child perched on his lap, was splayed on her belly. He leafed through his picture books of World War Two, until he found a photo of Hitler taken at a similar, if not identical, angle.

Hitler, seen from a distance in full face, in this case sitting on a picnic blanket with several young women. Dr Hake took a pencil and aged this face by thirty years. He sketched pouches under the eyes, he doubled the chin, and drew a new hairline, leaving the parting on the far right side.

Then he compared his drawn-over Hitler with the photo of Carl Bauer. His Most Artful Conspirator's intentions aside, age had provided Hitler with the perfect disguise, thickening him into a well-stuffed, elderly man. More flesh padded his nose and jawline than Dr Hake would have predicted. The ears were a bit baggier than in his youth, the lower lip drooped more conspicuously. Perhaps this made Carl Bauer so sure of his anonymity that he had dared to grow back the moustache that had always identified him. In Palmerston North, New Jersey, one hardly noticed it: a white toothbrush moustache, an old man's vanity. Yes, Hitler had always been vain.

The autumn storm that racked the city did not disturb Ronald. All night he sat and reflected at his desk where

70

he had once made love to Connie. His attention gave out all of a sudden, without warning. He slept, his handsome face crushed into the muscular crook of his arm.

He awoke in the morning, disoriented. He looked out of the window, and his confusion increased. The word 'Mortuary' was missing from the view. He climbed up on to his desk and looked down. The sign lay in the alleyway, nails ripped out and bent, a victim of the storm.

He returned to his desk, put his head down again and allowed his thoughts to prowl through the terrain they had staked out during the night. They went further afield; he daydreamed.

He was driving up a hill on a very bad road. The mud was splattering his canary yellow sports car; the doors were going to be filthy. The road was lined with pedestrians, dressed unbelievably poorly and looking miserable, probably because of the road conditions. The road led steeply uphill. He put his hand on the gear-stick and went down into first. The car protested, and then continued, slowly; he wasn't driving much faster than the pedestrians. At that tempo, he had nothing to do, and out of boredom he inspected them. He saw their faces. They were dark-skinned people, and their eyes were bright with misery. He rolled down his windshield and listened to what they were saying. He could only make out a humming, like static. But then their thoughts began to play across their eyes, action on two little television screens. They were thinking about having sex with their neighbours, strangling old aunts, consuming tons of forbidden fruit. Suddenly the images changed. He saw himself in their eyes, and their faces were turned to him with adulation. His excitement affected his foot, which pressed down hard on the gas pedal, so that the car suddenly picked up speed. His excitement bore down on him, like a weight on his back. He was leaning forward, almost bent in half over the steering wheel, while the car roared along the line of pedestrians, and suddenly he reached the top of the incline and saw two crucifixes stuck in the ground there. The weight on his shoulders became ever heavier and he felt the roughness of the steering wheel in his hand and recognized that it was made of wood. It was a long piece of wood, and he'd been dragging it along on his back.

Ronald snapped out of his fantasy with a start.

He put his fist to his chest and struck himself three times. 'Please, Lord, forgive me – I have blasphemed. Pretty please, forgive me, Lord. Pretty please, with sugar on top.'

Ronald was terrified.

5

The morning after Carl Bauer landed in the hospital, Connie followed an impulse she recognized as peculiar, given the family tragedy: she dressed to the nines in one of her mother's old floral silk dresses, added new stockings and her best pumps. She was annoyed to find Ronald's office door locked. After she presumed that no one was there, she knocked viciously. Then she heard the rustle of paper, the sound of books thudding, a drawer slammed. He came to the door, his eyes dull with fatigue, his clothes wrinkled, and smelling musty.

Connie frowned at him. She felt he should not lock doors. After all, he was not evasive. He had worried less than she about being caught at a love affair. She took this to be proof of a clear conscience. Why lock the door?

'The cleaning lady was trying to get in here this morning, and I wanted to sleep. I worked all night, I'm working at my new book. About pious people with secrets. What the secret means to the soul. With several new poems,' he said, and added plaintively, 'I slept on the desk.'

He stepped back. 'Come in.' He closed the door behind them and asked, 'You have any secrets I can use as a case study?'

'Secrets! No. I don't have time to have secrets. My father's ill.'

Then she told him the news, that her father was in the hospital. His response touched her, deepened her feelings of love, made her forgive his odour. She admired the high colour in his cheeks as he became agitated. 'What! He isn't going to die, is he?'

He comprehended the ease with which a body of research can disappear. Especially secrets. When the vessel bearing them is gone, the secrets disappear too. Even the spirit, the memory of that person, contain no mention of what he felt necessary to hide. It's their secrets that distinguish one man from the next. And the Church and the psychiatrists with their thieves' Latin, keeping all those trophies for themselves.

'Darling, I hope he won't die,' she said. 'But you can come and visit him if you like.'

'I would like. I insist.'

But that night Connie did not visit Carl Bauer either. Ronald couldn't get over how pretty she looked in all those flowers, with those tiny pumps. He just had to show her the sunset over Fifth Avenue. They passed a church with a sign 'Father Fowler Is NOT In' and Ronald asked, 'Do you want to go inside?' She did not. He persisted. 'Do you believe?'

'Not really.'

'Why do you go then?'

'For the children.'

'You think they profit from it?'

'It gives them morals.' She laughed nervously.

'Watch this,' he said. He wondered whether he could impress her. He stood on the sidewalk, folded his hands and chanted a poem he had written to annoy his roommate at school.

'Strato cumulus – !
Cirro Stratus,
Cumulus cirro stratus
Cirro-velum.

Mammalus cumulus – !
Cirro-nebula cirro-fillum
Mammatocumulus
Cirro-velum.

Nephelococcygia.'

Just as he'd predicted, blasphemy made Connie shriek with laughter. Stanislav didn't care enough about the Church to make fun of it. And then Ronald proved to be a man with talent for sexual variety. As a kind of foreplay, he bought her a cardigan to match her dress at a fashionable store. Stanislav would have gone mad about the cost, scolded about the lunacy of free enterprise that persuades people they need something they don't need, especially from Fifth Avenue. He would have taken his date to a used-book store down on Fourteenth Street and bought her a good novel. Whereas Ronald paid discreetly, excusing himself from Connie and then arranging everything with the saleslady at a distance. And he hated novels.

This was, for Connie, the erotica of normalcy. She rang Gerda and told her, 'I'm going to be home very late. We have an emergency down here.' She didn't come home all night.

The family squirmed in agony like a wounded slug.

6

There were so many spectres haunting New York. The Cuban politician, asked like a child what he would wish for if the good fairy granted him three wishes, replied: his first wish would be to see an atom bomb drop on New York; his second wish would be to see a second atom bomb drop on New York; his third and final wish would be to see a third and final atom bomb drop on New York. Meanwhile, someone was placing modest bombs on the city subways, randomly blowing up just one yellow laminated straw seat at a time, and any person sitting on it. In the eye of a construction boom, the politicians moved buildings and streets around, like poltergeists. Inside the suburban house on River Avenue there was a haunting absence: the absence of a past; the brooding presence of the absent past. With Carl Bauer gone, the clocks chimed and saluted, the checker sets held their positions on the wooden front, the recliner remained at Up, the children leaning carelessly against it were scolded for recklessness by Gerda, all night long Happy's tail thumped sociably in his doggie bed. He knew something was changed in the house, could not tell what, interpreted the change as something positive and, too weak and satisfied to get up, he rang his tail on the cushion.

Over in Manhattan, Connie awoke at dawn in Ronald's

bed and looked around at her surroundings. He was awake too. He had never spent an entire night with a woman before. Fatigue had dragged him down into the depths of sleep the night before, drowned him before he could hold on to the body going down with him. Within hours, the strangeness of sharing his bed had forced him to bob to consciousness again. She was lying on her back and he saw her cat's eyes peering out from between his sheets, with a strange glimmer.

Ronald pretended to sleep and felt her hand stroking the sheet. He guessed she was marvelling at the obvious expense: satin sheets. Then she lay still and looked around her and he knew that she must notice the perfect combination of beiges and creams (arranged, Ronald had told her the night before, by a real interior decorator when he'd moved down from New Haven. 'We've always had interior decorators – we're an old American family').

He saw her turn her head for an instant in the direction of his wardrobe, and then look away quickly. She seemed very discreet. Discretion is sometimes present as a reflex among those who themselves have secrets to guard, thought Ronald. The reflex can be suspended, but only through conscious effort. He watched her: she was looking at the ceilings, at the antique love seat, the immaculate wall-to-wall, and she dwelled on his new toaster and washing machine, recognizing their value. He stirred carefully. She turned towards him, looked at his eyes, and, taking his head in both hands, she whispered to him, 'Neatness is a wonderful quality. Ronald? You are really tidy.'

'Any objections?' he answered, smiling, without opening his eyes.

'My mother celebrated order so vigorously that even Nature took fright. During the autumn, the leaves of

77

our trees fell on to the neighbour's lawn. In the winter, the snow drifted off our property and we never lifted a shovel. But this – is wonderful.'

Meanwhile, over in New Jersey, Gerda packed a suitcase for the children. 'No, you're not going to school. If Connie doesn't come home, and Mr Bauer's away, then I decide what happens here. And my decision is: your father must decide. I'm just the maid. I have enough to do.'

She didn't know which bus to take to the city. The children tried to tell her, but she just ignored them. 'God gave you legs,' she said. She was not much taller than Dicker. She dragged the case and set the pace, trudging along the big naked road Carl Bauer's ambulance had taken. They crossed the bridge to Manhattan, high up over the river, the late-November sun flashing through the clouds and the wind thundering in the steel girders. From there they descended into Washington Heights, with its narrow cluttered streets, the kosher garbage on the sidewalks and a synagogue. Dicker stopped walking and stared at the slovenly grey building, with litter covering the steps.

'Slowpoke,' called Sally.

'Imagine,' he said. 'If we set foot in there it's a mortal sin. All we have to do is go up the stairs, and step over the threshold – hell for ever.'

Gerda turned back to him, yanked his arm and pulled. 'Stop your nonsense and hurry,' she said.

When they reached Stanislav's esteemed university, her legs sped up. This way, that way, she dragooned them through the corridors, hysterical with contempt. Finally they reached his laboratory, and she deposited them on two hard chairs there, told them to pray for their grandfather, among the test-tubes. She found the smell despicable, worse than garlic; she was sensitive about foreign smells. She dashed off without waiting for Stanislav to put in his bedraggled appearance.

He was roaming the halls, as always bent almost double, his hands twiddling behind his back, in what he called 'Socrates' thinking position', the pace. His children watched him enter the office, turn around it once without spotting them, and then barge back out to the halls. He was thinking about complex carbohydrate. On his umpteenth spin past them, he noticed that he was not alone. He stopped short, stared, and finally chuckled, touched by his own absent-mindedness.

He patted them once on the cheek nearest him, his hand wrinkled, weak, smelling of chemicals. He remarked, 'You've come to visit me!'

'We've come,' said the practical Sally, 'to stay with you.'

'Stay with me!' he cried. 'But that's impossible! I have so much work to do. I can't be bothered with you.'

'Mama didn't come home last night,' Sally plodded on. 'We think she's going to get married.'

'She already is married,' Stanislav replied carelessly. 'Please, children. You'll have to go back to your grandfather. I'll take you to the bus stop.'

They sat patiently in the lab chairs waiting for Stanislav to come to his senses.

'We didn't go to school today,' ventured Dicker. 'And we haven't eaten anything for hours.'

'Grandfather is in the hospital!' Sally remembered then. 'But still, wouldn't it be nice to go to the movies?'

Dr Miele felt the nature of the pathologists' line of work made them less vain than other physicians, who strolled through the jungle of humanity weeding and hoeing, occasionally shooting a bird, and imagining they were responsible for all that flourished there in the first place. Dr Miele strolled around the autopsy room, cigar in his mouth, sharpening his knife. His cadaver lay on the table tenth from the left, with a bit of time to kill, as long as Miele was expounding. He had a theory: different personalities were attracted to different fields. The surgeons were sunny boys, superficial bastards, instant gratifiers, the vainest and most mistake-prone of the lot.

Next to the obstetricians, Dr Guttenberg interjected.

Dr Miele agreed, and added that he had refused to have children because he didn't ever want to be at the mercy of an obstetrician. Dr Bauer and Dr Guttenberg stood with their backs to the swinging doors of a refrigerator room that ought to open any minute. But the Diener was obviously taking his time bringing in what looked like a double suicide beneath E-train wheels. 'Dieners are lazy as a way of life,' said Dr Miele, and inspected the blade of his knife. Still no good. 'That's why they're called Dieners. Isn't that German for servant, Dr Bauer?'

'You may as well go for a walk, with Dr Hake. I know how you like going for walks,' said Dr Guttenberg. 'You could take him over to the clinic and have a free Wassermann test.'

Quickly Dr Bauer opened her own instrument case, a rough pine box that looked like a miniature public coffin, and joined Dr Miele strolling, talking business and sharpening their instruments on regulation kitchen sharpeners, their elbows flying in circular motions. And the conversation swung back and forth, back and forth.

'According to your theory, Dr Miele, who becomes a pathologist?'

'Oh-ho,' said Dr Guttenberg.

'Thieves, in the fifteenth century. Body-snatchers, with insatiable curiosity, today, mere cynics,' said Dr Miele, 'those who know a thing or two about human nature and don't want to know any more, those who don't care about getting praise and fancy liquor from grateful patients.

'You're very quiet today,' he addressed Dr Bauer as he inspected his knife again, and muttered, 'Fine.' He went over to the cadaver.

'You know I don't have any opinions of my own. Opinions are something too complex, too ephemeral for me,' Dr Bauer said. 'I admire those who have them tremendously. My father is ill, you know. He had a coronary two nights ago.'

'No one's immune. I hope you got a good cardiologist. Always check his thumbs. If he has more than one milli-metre tennis callus, find someone else. Do you think it's cold in here? I bet the heating's broke again. Here comes your post. I'm going to start mine. Look, here's our Sunny Jim, hullo, Dr Hake. Are you going to say us your poem, Dr Hake?'

'I'm not in the mood.'

'That's all right. I don't like pottery anyway.'

'You mean poetry.'

'I can't help it. I think it's for ladies.'

'Do you like music?' asked Dr Hake.

'Yeah, sure.'

'Same thing.'

'I like tangos.'

They held their knives up.

'Over at Park Lane they're sharpening electrically now,' said Dr Miele enviously.

★

81

The temperature in the morgue sank slowly throughout the morning. By the time the pathologists were on the last leg of their cases in the autopsy room, their fingers were white and stiff. They could hear the secretaries arguing vigorously about nothing, like birds who scold to keep warm. Dr Miele reiterated for the nth time his theory that there should be a Nobel Prize given for curiosity, and that the sixteenth-century pathologist and grave-robber Dr Vesalius should get the first one posthumously. Usually the others just rode out Dr Miele when he was on to Vesalius, but this morning Dr Guttenberg was cold enough to contradict him. He said in his opinion Nobel prizes should only be given for achievement peculiar to human beings, and even dogs were curious. The only difference between man and animal, said Dr Bauer, speaking up for the first time, her voice lilting despite the cold, is that man knows there's no hope.

After Stanislav discovered the children in his laboratory he had no choice but to provide for their amusement. 'Your mother is impossible,' he said. 'I detest her, really.' He fussed around with his test-tubes, muttering to himself in Polish. They stayed in their seats, grateful that no one else was there to see him make a fool of himself, talking to his chemicals in that ungodly language, his weak hands meddling with the bunsen-burner. Their anxiety paid off; presently something went flying, and he looked with stupid dismay at the spill and the broken glass and repeated, 'I detest her, really.' Footsteps sounded in the hall: two technicians entered, one with a cloth, the other with a broom.

He made room for them to clean up, watching with

satisfaction, his hands twiddling behind his back. As soon as they were gone he said, 'It's useless working with you two completely unable to amuse yourself. Why don't you read something? You just sit there and drive every normal person to make mistakes.'

He left the room without a word. They followed him to the secretary's office where they expected him to complain about this situation but all he said to the secretary was, 'I'm taking the children out for a while.'

She didn't hear him, she was listening to a radio jingle. It was her mid-morning prerogative.

'Advertising executives are people on welfare. They do nothing and get paid for it,' said Stanislav, pointing to the radio. He spoke for the benefit of the children. 'America has the most extensive peacetime welfare system in history. In the rest of the world they have beggars. Here they have advertising agencies. Anyone who works there is actually just a welfare sop.'

'Your father's a genius,' the secretary said to Dicker, turning down the volume. 'Are you going to be a genius like your dad?' Dicker grunted. 'And win a Nobel Prize?'

'I guess we're going to the movies now,' Sally said.

'Gosh, Dr Reich, your children are adorable. I'm sure you're going to have a wonderful time with them, get out of this place for once. Have some fun. Not always science – ' She wrinkled her nose and the children laughed dutifully.

He took them to the next liquor store. They waited outside the shop window. Its venetians were drawn, but the red colour of the interior walls seeped out through the slats. When the door opened, the light from inside shimmering red like vermouth spilled into the street, on to their legs, and they gulped the air, inhaling greedily the sweet smell of cheap liquor. Finally he emerged gripping a paper bag by the neck and they proceeded up Broadway to the next cinema in time for the mid-morning showing.

Stanislav paid for tickets without enquiring about the programme. Dicker was concerned. The film had Hiroshima in the title and then several French words the children did not understand. Dicker wielded his *Film Rating* published by the Catholic Legion of Decency. He always carried this pamphlet on his person, but his copy was outdated, and the film was not listed. ' "Hiroshima" – it'll be a war movie,' said Dicker, 'so it has to be family rated.'

They sat down in the middle of the cinema, the children equipped for a long winter with pounds of junk food. Stanislav found his children irritating; they didn't take film seriously enough. They snacked loudly, rustled and tore the wrappers, and shoved the packets back and forth. He couldn't hear the soundtrack.

The children twitched and giggled. The film was about a couple in love. Before long, this man and woman began to kiss. It was no ordinary kiss. It was an incomprehensibly boring kiss that never stopped. Sally was willing to wait it out. Dicker panicked.

'This can't possibly be family rated,' he said. 'I'm sure it's limited.'

The kiss became ever more elaborate.

'This is condemned, I'm sure of it. We're seeing a film that's condemned!' Dicker said. 'We better leave.'

'Oh shut up, Dicker,' Sally said. 'Just have some popcorn. They'll stop this soon enough.'

Stanislav offered no advice. He had shut them out of his consciousness.

Dicker stood up, a tiny black figure against the huge

kissing faces. 'I'm getting out of here!' he said. 'You're sinning, Sally, a mortal sin.'

'It doesn't say on your list, Dicker, sit down,' she pulled at him.

He tore away.

Light flickered in the back of the cinema as he slipped through the door. Sally sat back in her seat and waited for a more interesting scene.

Dicker hadn't been gone for more than a minute when the overhead lights in the cinema went on. The man and woman continued to kiss but it was harder to see them. A few people turned around and stared. Suddenly a man in a suit ran down to the big screen. Tears streamed down his cheeks. Sally was astonished at Dicker's power.

The man started shouting to cover the great distance between the screen and the last aisle. 'Ladies and gentlemen! The Heights Theatre down the street has been bombed! Until we know why, we're going to have to close up.'

People stood up and grumbled about their money and morning wasted.

He ran out again. The curtains slammed shut like book covers on the still kissing pair. Stanislav and Sally found Dicker being gluttonous with popcorn in a corner of the front hall. Stanislav refused to leave without getting his tickets refunded, and they joined a long queue of fun-lovers shouting at the cashier.

Broadway was decked out in afternoon tabloids bearing the news. Stanislav seemed angry. 'Just because one movie theatre is bombed, he thinks it has to happen to his theatre!' He clutched his paper bag and walked very fast and bent over, and they had a hard time keeping up with him. His face brightened and his walk slowed when he remembered how he was going to solve a nasty problem about complex carbohydrate. 'We don't even have a television,' Dicker mourned.

At the City Morgue, business began to register a boom. The first ambulance arrived, bringing the bodies still in one piece, the attendants stacking them in the basement after the refrigerators were full. 'Darn, it's cold in here,' they complained. 'Be glad,' replied the technician. 'It's just pure luck, or a thank the Lord that the heat broke. If you knew.'

'Goina be a bit a' puzzle work for yous,' said the officer in charge of personal possessions, looking for recognizable objects. The next load arrived in crates labelled 'Arms', 'Legs'.

Upstairs in the secretaries' office, the news of a death rarely caused a sensation. Yet Alice became melancholic when she heard the numbers of children involved. Her sorrow was infectious. The staff of the morgue gathered in the office, and when the room was full they said nothing. Then one recognized that Dr Hake and Dr Bauer were missing. Distress at the deaths of so many innocent people was heightened by the suspicion that Dr Hake and Dr Bauer were somewhere having a good time. 'If those two don't show up soon, heads are going to roll here,' promised Dr Guttenberg to himself. In fact, they were down in the tunnels again, running the bases inside Connie's racoon coat.

Over in New Jersey, Gerda was hunched over the dining-room table, picking at her paralysed radio dial with a screwdriver. She jabbed and lifted. All of a sudden, the dial budged. She stared, frightened at what she'd done. Then, quickly, she took the radio into her kitchen, plugged it in, and turned the dial this way and that. In these delicious meanderings she suddenly heard the news about sixty-seven innocents dying in a movie theatre over in Manhattan. She held on to the kitchen sink, started to turn the radio off, and thought better of it. All alone, she wore a look of stubborn decision. She heard it all, about the bomb, the dead children, and the casualties fighting for life at City hospitals.

For no apparent reason, the shade on the kitchen window began to swing. She saw that the window behind it was closed. It swung until it thudded lightly against the pane. She counted, one, two, three . . . Sixty-seven times the shade thudded against the pane, and then it hung still again. The dead are passing through my kitchen, thought Gerda, and she knelt down and prayed for them. She didn't think much about it. It was like in the First World War. She'd had constant window banging in her convent room.

Later, she realized she was neglecting her duty to Carl Bauer. He must be protected from the bad news. Crime depressed him so. She hurried to get ready for her evening visit, packing a picnic hamper with his dinner. His black Buick stood in the garage. She had never learned to drive. The master and mistress had argued about it. Eva said in America women, and even maids, drove cars, it would be very useful if Gerda could drive. But Carl said Never. Gerda was firm on her feet, measuring distances in rosaries. It was two and a half rosaries to the hospital in a terrible rush, worried that he had been informed.

He had not heard a thing. He was sleeping on his back, his hands on top of the covers. Sacrifice lay ahead for Gerda: she'd have to stay up all night if necessary, keep someone from tattling. She posted herself at the door, and when a nurse came in to measure his usuals, Gerda muttered to her, 'Don't say nothing to him about the bomb, miss, it will just upset him.'

The nurse answered, 'All right, darling, don't you worry.' And then she addressed the man to whom Gerda had dedicated her entire life, for whom she had turned down Gerhardt, a hunchbacked chauffeur. The nurse lifted Mr Bauer's precious hand from the bed, as if it meant nothing, slipped her fingers under his pulse and said, 'Hi there, Carl, honey, how you feeling?'

Public tragedies require fierce national concentration. When it begins to get boring, it's even better. Then ritual and repetition creep in, and ritualized boredom has always drawn the masses. Who and why, the media intoned. Why me? Why then? the victims asked. It was Friday the thirteenth, that's why. It was a film about Sindbad the Sailor, that's why. I forgot to pet Wolfgang, my terrier dog, in the morning, that's why. Lessons To Be Drawn: The danger of public enclosures. The danger of the deranged. The strangeness of the arraigned. Very quickly, they had him, a nice Jewish boy, fresh from Yeshiva, and smelling of kosher pickles. He was seen hovering around the bombed theatre, counting victims with a toy pistol, which wasn't against the law. Asked politely by a passing cop, he confessed everything in time for the evening news. The cops had a disappointment coming: the kid didn't know his gelignite from his trinitrotoluene, not to mention, on his own pistol, his cock from his butt.

The pathologists knew everything at a glance: an explosion. The reflex frown at impact turned out masks, charcoal-black faces with white wrinkles and crow's feet. The explosion followed by fire. Some of what wasn't torn apart burned quickly, leaving the body in the boxing-position. What wasn't burned, drowned in carbon monoxide released by the fire. What didn't suffocate, or burn, and could still move and reason, panicked, ran itself into a corner, got itself trampled. Oh, well. To work.

The temperature in the morgue reached, in the course of the afternoon, the optimum four degrees celsius necessary for preserving the dead, so the corpses could be brought in and stored directly in the autopsy room. The pathologists and dieners wore their winter coats and scarves. One might have taken the colourful crowd that worked beneath the closed skylight for one of the Old Master's winter markets. Everyone was performing some part of the same transaction: opening and closing, handing over, weighing, commenting, exchanging. After a case was finished, the pathologist put all the organs in a plastic bag, dropped the bag into the cavity of the torso and sewed it up, with big, careless stitches. And had a rest before taking on the next one. The police did a lot of the puzzle work, matching up likely body parts.

Dr Hake and Dr Bauer were in the thick of things. They had returned from their tropical hideaway just in time, claiming they'd gone, separately, to look up two separate cases in the medical library when they heard the news – separately. They had met at the morgue entrance. In fact, down in the tunnels, they'd heard the racket of undertaking students enter the Practical Year room in such numbers that they knew there must be a mass exitus. They had run through the tunnels, surfaced in the main building and staged their arrival. While Dr Hake donned his surgical clothes, he thought, 'Carl Bauer's reaction to this news will provide an important piece of testimony to the perfection of his contrition, showing whether there are altered vital states in large territories of his conscience.'

And he determined to visit Carl Bauer that same day and take him the news.

Drs Bauer and Hake left the morgue as the inmates of the male ward were having their afternoon drug cocktails. They heard the tinkle of her heels, and ignored the slower pedalpoint of a man's heavy Oxfords. Thunder of their feet, ringing of their cups, joyful joyful joy of man's desiring.

Ronald put his arm around her. The patients screamed in lust and fury. She pulled away from him. 'It only antagonizes them. They can't get out, the poor things.'

'I don't think they're so poor,' Ronald said. 'Three meals a day. Look at all that energy!'

'That's the energy of the insane,' she replied. 'I have it too.'

'Maybe it's having secrets that makes people insane. Like tertiary syphilis. If the patient had admitted his illness at the onset, he would have received treatment, and would never have become so ill. And imagine, he infects his loved ones because he won't tell them the truth. Secrets do a lot of damage. Listen to these nuts.'

'Well, shall we get rid of our common secret? We can call your sister, and tell my father,' she said lightly. 'Because otherwise we'll get locked up with my admirers, at this rate. At least we'll be together.'

He was too infatuated to protest: why, why wouldn't she tell him her secret, and spare him the necessity of figuring it all out behind her back! Why did he like her so much, he continued, chastizing himself. He liked her despite her past, and despite her car. He realized with a shock that Connie drove a car he considered antithetical to all that he respected – a pigeon-grey wreck of a Ford subcompact. Nor did she drive in a feminine, delicate,

90

cautious and slightly clumsy way. No, she drove like an ordinary cabbie, she kept her index finger on the wheel and, guided by this one digit, she swerved and snuck, careened and braked.

'Were you in Germany when they began to persecute the Jews?' he asked her profile.

'No, not really.'

'Do you know anyone who believed in killing them?'

'Who killed the Jews?' chanted Connie.

> 'I, said the sparrow,
> With my bow and arrow.
> I killed the Jews.'

'I'm serious! Or, did you ever see anyone die?'

'Oh yes!' laughed Connie. 'As the fly – '

> 'I saw them die,
> With my little eye.
> I saw the Jews die.'

'You really don't want to talk about it, do you?'

'No, I really don't. Let's talk about bone reconstruction. Let's talk about Ronald, Dr Hake.'

He sat sullenly, refusing to talk for the rest of the journey.

She comforted him. 'Look, the whole trouble with people is: every time they open their mouths, out comes a word.'

As they neared the suburban hospital where Carl Bauer was incarcerated for his heart attack, Ronald struggled to focus his thoughts on the inquiry. This latest crime could be divided into two experiences for Hitler: it was (a) a bombing, and (b) a bit of genocide. He needed to see exactly how the news of both (a) and (b) affected the former Führer. As (a), it must elicit a slight paranoia, at least. The last bomb explosion he had experienced in 1944 had been directed against him. Both timpani were shredded. As for the psychological impact, Hitler had claimed that his surprise survival proved that a Higher Force was looking out for him. Despite this claim of confidence, Hitler had, by all accounts including Mussolini's, become very paranoid and mistrustful afterwards. There was a scene over tea where he wouldn't stop kvetching about his officers; it had embarrassed his guest, the Duce. Ronald intuited that the bomb must have left traces, a scab. Prodded by the reminder of today's bombing, (a), the wound would peel open and bleed anew. As for (b). If Hitler had a clear conscience, he would not be unduly upset at the news of mass incineration that was not the slightest his responsibility.

Connie drove into the hospital parking lot and noticed that Ronald looked awfully grim for a hospital visitor. 'I'd appreciate it if you could just fake a good mood,' she said. Ronald always frowned when he concentrated. And he knew he had to look sharp now. He regretted that he had only taken one psychology course at Princeton.

7

For PJ, life had taken a turn for the less interesting. These days she could no longer expect to see Carl Bauer trotting by with Happy. Instead, she saw Gerda, who had no talent for dogs, if you asked the neighbours. Gerda always walked the creature around the same block. He had no opportunity to·expand his domain (age scarcely affected territorial ambitions), and she set such a pace that even the fastest Happy – and he was, at his age, a slow Happy – had no time to sniff out the location where his mark could make a difference.

PJ sat in her kitchen window, her chin on her hand, allowed her shellacked black hair to fall over her face like a curtain, and behind it she appeared as a daydreaming seventeen-year-old. She remembered arriving in Europe feeling utterly frustrated at how little she had learned about her guest, despite spending all that time together on the boat, over dinner, dancing, casino. She could reconstruct every minute with Carl and had him before her now, leaning against the boat railing, staring at the rapidly approaching coast of Europe. His face was grey and hard as a boulder, with the red sun burning on it. After seven days at sea, she had come to know only two sides of him: his reserve, and his intense, attractive sadness. Sitting in her kitchen window, six years later,

PJ concluded about herself, sadness in men always makes me go nuts.

Every time she became explicit to herself about longing for Carl, PJ writhed emotionally, and felt there was no escape from her own desire. She became helpless and frantic. Usually this ended with her turning on the television to some over-emotional soap opera and weeping her eyes out at the newest development. (It could be anything, happy, sad, dramatic, dull, the degree of emotion was all that mattered. But the suds only formed when she could mix in the awareness that Carl was only a few metres away.) And today, knowing that Carl lay at the far side of the suburb where he was probably preoccupied with his own health – surely not thinking of her! – a soap opera would do nothing for PJ. So she tried something different.

PJ primped. She fixed her face, beat her hair into a starker fluff, and dressed for an Occasion in her best polyester. She threw a shawl over her shoulders (he would have protested, 'You'll catch your death, my precious child') and trotted over to the Bauers'. She knew exactly where Gerda kept her spare key, in that place she trusted and respected like a grave – the garbage bin.

With a matter of factness that would convince any spying neighbours of her rights, PJ retrieved the key and entered the Bauers' house. Once inside, her head began to throb with excitement. She wondered briefly whether she might not have a stroke. It would be disagreeable to have a stroke all alone in someone else's living room. Stratford had had his at a shopping centre. He couldn't have had more attention when he departed. The sensation of pressure on her temples ceased when she saw all those clocks, and they reminded her she had only two hours before Gerda returned. But for those hours she could do anything she liked. 'Use your imagination, gal,' she told herself. 'Look the house over, consider the redecoration problems you'll face. Prepare ahead of time. The clocks will have to go. Every last one of them. Hate the darn things.'

She sat down on the sofa next to Carl's recliner, put her hand on the recliner arm and remembered sitting with Carl like that in the lobby of the hotel in Strasbourg. 'Where's Eva?' PJ asked again, six years later, putting the same glitter of concern in her voice, which was impossible to call artificial. In fact, she *was* worried. At the same time, she was *not* worried. PJ imagined Carl freshly showered, wearing his Hoboken suit. 'She's not feeling well, so she's a little slow.'

'And you, Carl?'

'I'm fine, thank you. Here she comes.'

PJ swung her head and looked at Eva's photo on the television. Looking her age. She was in her early fifties. Her neck sagged, and she had quite a lot of weight to carry around on her delicate ankles. She wore everything tight and bright anyway. And she had such pride. Dear God: pride is what makes women attractive, and either you have it or you don't. Her face was in three-quarter profile, girlish and with eyes utterly without expression, eyes blue and blank as patches of velvet.

'Should we get going?' Eva said, without enthusiasm.

They took the tram to the woods, and from there they walked to the river bank. On the other side, Germany lay quiet, uneventful, with the stores full of cuckoo clocks. PJ hopped up from the sofa and began to pace around and around the dining-room table, imitating their slow, pleasant walk along the Rhine river. The Rhine represented passions. All the Hudson did was keep New York from

New Jersey. No one had ever written a poem about that. Carl kept peering across the wide, boiling body of water. He had become uncommunicative again. Eva too had lost her butterfly prettiness. She put her fists to her breast in an old-fashioned gesture of emotion. Pacing around the table, PJ imitated her. It felt nice. She tried to feel emotional about the river, but all she could think of was how swell it would be to buy a cuckoo clock. 'We can cross over to the other side,' she said to Eva's picture. 'There's a bridge. Then we're in Germany.'

She returned to the recliner, patted the arm and wheedled, 'And then you can speak German without anyone thinking you're a foreigner.'

How well PJ remembered Carl's expression, how the dagger of his glare sliced into her, driving, splitting her flesh. Stratford was even-tempered, his nature flat as the Hudson at its widest, where he was born. She had never been so deliciously reprimanded in her whole life. PJ had to sit down on the sofa again; her breathing came in bubbly fits.

PJ looked at a clock. There was time for her favourite scene, which had taken place the following afternoon. Standing up near the sofa, PJ put her hand on the shoulder of the recliner, pretending it was Carl's head. Next to her, on the sofa, Eva was unconscious. 'Calm down, Carl, please. Eva will be all right. Maybe she just needs the rest.' She stood, her eyes closed, and luxuriated, spinning the moment out longer and longer, as if it were gossamer,

until the clocks rang and she had to run out.

Carl Bauer was on the post-op floor. The nurses no longer took any interest in him, proof that he was out of danger. Three times a day, Gerda brought him meals from home in a big basket.

The orderly complained about the hospital food himself but he resented this show of protest. He delivered the meals, banged them down on the patient's table and watched as Gerda struggled to remove them again. Before his eyes the tiny woman, buzzing with fury, staggered off with the tray, placing it at the far corner of the room on a chest of drawers, scowling at the smell. The orderly stayed and watched as she unpacked her hamper, arranging what she had brought on to the table as formally as possible, on her own dishware, with a fresh linen napkin, and the Bauers' best silver.

'I'll come and pick up the tray in half an hour,' the orderly said. 'That long you'll have to live with it. Rules.'

This ritual had just been re-enacted as Connie and Ronald entered. Gerda was standing at the foot of the patient's bed, watching him. Carl was looking at his plate sadly, the sadness caused by the juxtaposition of his condition (helpless and ill) with the sight of buttered potatoes, creamed spinach, bit of onion, slice of roast. Gerda went to such trouble, but he couldn't enjoy it, it only made him feel decrepit.

He recognized Connie's footsteps. 'Papa?' she said from the door. He flinched. He refused to look up at her.

'You're late. Too late. I don't want to see you,' he said to the spinach. 'My only daughter,' he said to the meat. 'Eva always said you would betray me if you had to,' to the gravy puddle.

Then he registered the other footsteps, virile in their slow approach, and he looked up. He forgot his confinement, and his face brightened. The white moustache that crowned everything he said bobbed. He was so pleased to see a man he respected.

'Dr Hake,' he said, 'do come in. I suppose you've an idea why my only daughter didn't visit me earlier.' He was not being facetious or ironic. He expected an underling, like a favourite lieutenant, to explain his daughter to him. But Ronald's power of interpretation failed him. He felt utterly found out. The memory of Connie beneath him in the hot, damp tunnel invaded him frontally. He blurted out the only excuse he could think of. 'Because there's been a terrible tragedy.'

Gerda gasped. The young man was going to do a lot of harm.

'What's happened!' asked Carl Bauer.

Gerda's gasp changed *en route* into a sigh. Well, if the young man felt it was important to tell Carl Bauer, he must have his good reasons.

Ronald was too addled to take note of Carl's reaction. He did not notice any involuntary movement, whether he shrank, whether sweat appeared on his forehead, whether he trembled. Instead, Ronald was remembering how certain words had lapped into his mouth from some hidden, dangerous spring, how they were part of his own panting, pushing up from the pillow of her body and then the billowing adoration he could not suppress. 'I love you.'

His face went bright red and he blurted, 'A bombing!' and he made the sign of the cross.

Carl Bauer followed suit.

'We wanted to pray with you,' Ronald finished.

'Let us pray,' said Carl Bauer.

When the orderly came to pick up the tray he found the patient had three visitors, two of them on their knees, the third one standing in front of Carl Bauer's bed. Their eyes were closed, their lips moving. The patient lay back on his pillow, staring at the cold food on his table, with an expression the orderly interpreted as post-op depression.

Later, Gerda and Connie left Ronald alone with Carl Bauer.

'Let the two gentlemen talk,' Gerda said. 'I'd like to water the flowers.' She meant the flowers on Eva's grave. 'I have to do everything.

'Look after Mrs Bauer.

'Look after Mr Bauer.

'Look after a house.

'Look after children.

'It was bad enough looking after you as a child. Pretending you were my own. I'm very tired of it. Drive carefully please.' They drove to the cemetery, a pretty place on a hill overlooking a garbage dump. 'When are you going to ask what I've done with your children?' asked Gerda. 'You don't even know where they are, do you. You think they're sitting at home, doing their homework. Well, you're wrong.' She flitted around the flowers. Whenever she passed the gravestone she stopped, read the inscription there and shook her head to show incomprehension. It read 'Eva Bauer, departed March 5, 1959, for the Valley of Love and Delight'.

'I don't know why Mr Bauer lets a Quaker mason decide what should be on his wife's tombstone. Valley. What valley?' She flew off, returned. 'Heaven is not a valley. Heaven is up there.' She pointed.

Ronald sat in a chair at the foot of the patient's bed. He began with (a): 'Presumably, they'll catch the person who set the bomb.'

'If they don't,' said Carl Bauer with new vitality, sitting upright in his bed, 'then God will catch him.'

'If he confesses his sin, then God will absolve him,' said Ronald. He took a chance. 'Let's not call him God. Let's call him, the Great Provider, the Marvellous Machinator.'

Carl Bauer replied coldly, 'What's wrong with saying God?'

'Well, I try not to, because then I automatically think of a man with a beard, who speaks with the birdies.'

Carl Bauer said nothing. Ronald tried (b).

'A mass death is something particularly terrible. And under such circumstances. Locked in. Panic. Suffocation. And then their bodies burned. Or do you think that it's possible that they somehow deserved it?'

Carl Bauer was very pale. 'What do you mean,' he said, 'deserved it? You mean, that they were sent to the inferno ahead of time, before death, damnation enforced possibly by someone with a funny beard? Who hates innocent bystanders? I don't know.'

'We live in order to sin, don't we,' said Ronald, consulting his hands. Strong hands, still there. He wasn't allowed to smoke in the hospital, dammit. His pipe knocked around in the breast pocket next to his heart. This was proving difficult. 'And then we die, that's the original sin we never lose. But some die in more horrible ways than others. I've learned that in my profession.'

'Have you?' said Carl Bauer. 'You seem to know a great deal about the different kinds of death.'

'Knowledge, knowledge,' said Ronald. He loved the sound of the word. 'Knowledge is what distinguishes us from the cud-chewers. I believe, by the way, that our God – the Force of Life – punishes those who presume to manipulate life – the murderers, and the doctors, and

100

the politicians. We pathologists only want to know why someone died, we want to know what goes on inside, we detest secrets.'

'There are different kinds of death – some have nothing to do with the body,' insisted Carl Bauer. But Ronald wasn't listening, he was watching his hands and developing his attack.

'And I see again and again that a secret behaves like a disease. It languishes: it poisons, or interferes with other functions. The uglier the secret, the uglier the havoc it wreaks on the person who harbours it. There are secrets which turn on thought, causing dementia, secrets which disseminate other secrets, so that the whole body is invaded and slowly all truth is replaced, and the patient is racked with the most ghastly pains as he retreats further and further from a state of grace. Self-deception, which works like degenerative heart disease, making the victim's soul necrotic and unable to love.

'As for love' (Ronald was being swept away by his own theory) 'then there are secret loves, which lead to sudden emotional death.

'Do you know that no dead man is uglier than the one who died during autoerotic excess, stuck on a machine, or tied up and strangled, because his secret suddenly comes to light, by killing him?'

Here Carl Bauer interrupted. 'I don't feel well, Ronald, I apologize. Believe me, I share your hatred of doctors. And scientists who interfere. We are of the same opinion, Ronald. That's very comforting.'

Ronald had been brought out of his train of thought. He fought for orientation – make him admit! – and then managed, 'And politicians, Mr Bauer? Do you despise the politicians?'

Carl Bauer looked at him. 'Yes, they are despicable,' he said. He leaned back against the pillow and closed his eyes. 'Just let me rest a minute,' he said. He fell asleep at once, his mouth hanging open. His body looked tiny in the white expanse of the hospital bed. Ronald felt his pulse. It was weak but steady, as if it were carefully bringing Carl Bauer along the boundary between sleep and death.

Later, Connie and Ronald returned to the morgue. Ronald immediately lit his pipe, but it did not relax him, and the drive was tense. Connie kept saying how glad she was that Ronald could talk to her father. Ronald was frustrated by her enthusiasm. 'We talked about religion,' he said, 'and – '

'Marvellous!' Connie said.

'Listen to me! He has a funny attitude towards religion.'

'We all do, dear.'

'I have a good idea that you don't even believe in God,' Ronald tried to provoke her.

'Yes. I believe in a god that looks like a newt. And when he croaks, bombs go up in cinemas.'

He couldn't tell whether she was teasing him. Not knowing angered him. He ground his teeth on his pipe until he bit through the mouthpiece, and the pipe fell on the dashboard, spilling tobacco everywhere. 'This car will smell of you for weeks,' Connie said with satisfaction.

Stanislav bought the children the *American Inquirer* because, he said, on a day like today, the papers were all alike, as in any totalitarian state. The news infuriated him: give the Press a bombing, and they take it as an excuse to drop every reference to the rest of the globe. He kept muttering 'morbid obsession'. But he saw that the papers gave the children something to do. He went to his lab. It was a Saturday, when the university was pleasantly empty. When he returned for lunch, the children staged a mutiny. They wanted a television. 'You have newspaper, you have books!' shouted Stanislav. 'What for do you need idiocy!' (idi' ossi) Then, alarmed at the hatred he saw in their eyes and in the recalcitrant set of their smooth lips, he phoned Connie.

'You sent the children here. You know I don't approve of television. You've obviously been systematically dunking them in it. TV works on their wits like formalin, it denatures the protein. And then you send them to me with their brains hard-boiled. Hellevision. The American pre-dead.' He was sobbing with rage.

The children shrieked and bounded around him. 'Yes! We want a television!'

Connie garbled, 'Look, it's just not true, we do not have a television, well, yes, we do, but we don't use it, it's hard to explain, you haven't visited – the easiest thing is: just don't believe them.

'But the point is, my father's still in the hospital. I can't expect Gerda to look after them. I'll buy you a television. Because I know it's the expense that makes you hate it. You don't want to spend the money. For a couple of hundred of dollars they'll keep amused, I'll pay. And you'll watch the evening news. You can see *Meet the Press* and *Stock Market Today*. You'll pick up tips.'

He hated capitalism, but as long as there was a stock market, he was going to keep his money there, instead of in a bank. The stock-market programme convinced him, since he had no one he could talk to about his investments. They met at a department store. It was the first time husband and wife had seen each other in months.

They acted nonchalant about it, hardly looking at each other, proceeding up to the fourth floor, which had six rows of televisions tuned to as many different channels, at least two to the 'morbid obsession'. Stanislav trembled. He kept his mouth shut, the last fragile barrier holding back the torrents of his fury.

To the children it was paradise. Rows and rows of the forbidden substance, low-brow entertainment. While the world was following its dreary routine, game-shows were being committed, acts of sport perpetrated, and nutty housewives exercised control over the national laugh.

Suddenly, high above the crackling and the yapping, a voice broke in, a male shriek, enraged. 'You hurry and serve me, so I can get out of here. Or do you take your time because I'm not a juvenile delinquent like you and your kind?'

The children raced through the aisle and saw him, Stanislav, small, bent, shabby, foreign, addressing the tall, young, sublime salesman who was standing next to him, but looking away, over the rows of the televisions, with an expression vacant as the panhandle.

They saw Connie appear at the far end of the row. Soundless, as though the volume of her footsteps had been turned off, she ran down the aisle. It took her ages to reach Stanislav, who had closed his eyes and was still ranting. She grabbed his arm. The children noted the gesture. They felt great relief and simultaneous wonder at the speed of the reconciliation. She was holding on as if she might never let go again.

She and Stanislav walked away quickly. He turned back his head and continued to rail at the salesman. 'Conceited fool! Arrogant juvenile! Delinquent!' The salesman shook his head, smiling grimly now, and as the children skirted him, admiring his loafers, adoring his occupation, he shuddered and said softly to himself, 'Boy oh boy, they forgot to gas you.'

They caught up with their parents on the other side of the glass stairwell door, where Stanislav had rolled up his sleeve and was staring at the five deep blue marks Connie's grip had left on his white arm. 'My dear, you yourself are one of these hoodlums,' he said.

'I'm taking Sally and Dicker with me,' she said. 'You're too addled to look after children. Making a scene like that. They ought to arrest you.'

'Will you drop me off at the lab?' he asked. 'I hope I don't get a blood infection.'

Connie drove. 'If I have an accident, it'll have to be called a homicide,' she said. She stepped on the brakes and watched him fly forwards. Her blonde curls bobbed attractively. He held on to the door handle. She looked down at his wizened white hand clutching the door handle and said, 'Do you honestly think holding on to the door handle will keep you from soaring through the windshield if I put my mind to it?' And as if to prove it, she nearly piled into the next car waiting at a red light.

The children huddled in the back. 'Don't tell me you're afraid to die!' she called over her shoulder. 'Dicker? Sally?' Sally sat up straight. If Mom wasn't afraid, then she wasn't going to be afraid. She looked contemptuously at Dicker, whose lips were moving, Holy Mary, mother of God, and Sally began to sing, in a high, soft, thrushlike voice, 'I wish I had that doggie in the window.'

After Connie dropped Stanislav off the tension left her and she regretted her behaviour. Instead of issuing an apology, she drove much too slowly. The children understood; they forgave her. She chatted with them

105

about school, and didn't tell them where she was driving. Soon she explained, 'We're still not finished at work. I'm going to drop you off at Ronald's house. He wanted you to be there in the first place. He says you can watch his television. It's colour.'

8

Carl Bauer was feeling stronger.
He sat up in bed and mixed watercolours on a palette. He enjoyed himself. He began to paint. He was absorbed in a picture of an alpine house surrounded by sheer, snow-covered mountains. The doctor swept in. 'Aha, feeling better, I see,' he said. 'What's this?'

He inspected the picture.

'An old mountain chalet in Colorado,' Carl Bauer replied.

When Connie returned to the morgue she found that Ronald had left for the research library. In fact Ronald had an appointment at church. A sign on the church bulletin board outside read, 'Father Fowler Is In'. Father Fowler was not expecting him, or anyone else. He was reading the London *Times* by flashlight in his half of the confessional. He was English, and he read only the London *Times*, although it always came five days late. He didn't mind about the delay. He put the paper down as quietly as possible when a customer came in. 'I don't want to make my confession, Father. I want to discuss an ethical problem I have.'

'Business is not exactly booming today. It must be sunny

skies out there. They come in when it rains. So go ahead. I
have time for you. And interest. Ethical problems are the
highlight of my job, you know. In the north of England,
I had the miners. They had good tales to tell. Here in
mid-town, people just use the name of the Lord in vain
about prices. So, tell me all about it.'

Ronald put his hands in the steeple position, and then,
since he couldn't see his hands in the dark, he pressed
the spire to his nose and smelled them. Formalin and
soap.

'I'm wondering, Father, about Adolf Hitler. The German. The Church teaches that Christ will welcome the
worst sinner back into the flock who repents. And Hitler
was in many ways a rather good man – he didn't drink,
he didn't curse, he didn't believe in murdering animals.
Is it possible to recapitulate for me what made him bad,
in the eyes of the Church?'

'You mean you want to know what is good about
Hitler, and what is bad about Hitler?'

'Yes, Father. If you don't mind.'

Father Fowler thought for a minute and said, 'This is
how I would summarize it. Bear in mind this is my
opinion, and not necessarily Rome's. And it's off the cuff.'
He slipped his voice into the slow gear, with long pauses
between important thoughts, that he usually reserved for
his sermons about Great Wickedness.

'I'll start with why he should be praised.

'One. In his public speeches he was courageous enough
to use the name of God. He trusted in the blessing of the
Creator.

'Two. He considered it his life's goal to destroy
Marxism.

'That, sadly, is all I can think of.

'And as to why he should not be praised. More occurs to me there.

'One. He advocated blind hate and the use of violence instead of spiritual weapons. He persecuted important Catholic men.

'Two. He advocated the cult of race and, by doing so, he rejected Christianity as a Jewish importation.'

Father Fowler paused, and then added with bitterness. 'And three. He was inconsequential, dreadfully in-con-se-quential! His friend Dr Goebbels, born a Catholic, married a divorced Protestant, and Hitler himself was the witness at this wedding.' Father Fowler stopped. Then he whispered, 'For a long time, much too long, he tolerated the presence of Röhm, a notorious homosexual!'

The priest paused. 'Is that what you wanted to know?'

'Yes.'

'Shall I hear your confession now?'

'No, Father. I'm in too much of a hurry.'

'That much of a hurry? Is the sun shining, do you have money jingling in your pocket that you want to spend? Is your girlfriend waiting for you? What's the hurry? If you wanna have your elbows on pillows, go to the Jesuits on Fifteenth Street, right?'

Ronald had already left for the morgue.

He remembered his daydream, and he remembered his attempts at trying to talk Carl Bauer out of using the name of the Lord. There had been something so simple, and therefore so convincing, about the German man's belief. He had felt ashamed. Walking back to the morgue, Ronald asked himself: what if Hitler *is* good because of the Church?

And he answered himself: then that would speak for the power of Catholicism and organized superstition. The

thought shocked him. I must find out! I must! But first he
had some autopsies to do.

'Over at Park Lane they're missing all these brains,' said
Dr Guttenberg.

'God must not have wanted pathologists mucking
around with them,' said Alice.

'But are they really gone?' asked Dr Hake.

'They allowed some young, handsome, conceited pathologist to organize the collection for an alcoholism study.
No surprise he loses the brains,' said Dr Guttenberg in the
young doctor's direction. 'I wouldn't blame it on God.'

'I think Dr Hake will agree with us,' said Alice from
behind her typewriter. 'As much as I respect you boys trying to clear up the cause of death and all that, I think maybe
the Creator doesn't like having brains sliced like any old
loaf of rye. And then being inspected in that condition by
people who have no relationship to Him at all.'

She stared at the autopsy report in her typewriter.

At that instant Dr Bauer walked in and said, 'Have
you heard that the Park Lane coroners have lost all the
brains? Trotsky's brain was lost too. It turned up after a
few decades.'

'Where?'

'About eight thousand miles away from the site of the
killing,' she said. 'In Bremen.'

'Where did you hear that?' asked Dr Hake.

'I don't know,' said Dr Bauer. 'Common knowledge
in Cincinnati, I suppose. Alice, you haven't baked cookies
for days!'

'No I haven't,' Alice sniffed. 'Dr Bauer, I've been way
out of sorts.' And she stuck on her earphones and typed
the pathologists out of her office.

'God,' she chastized Blessed, 'probably don't like theories about hisself and dissection.'

That day the children sat on Ronald's antique love seat and watched their eyes sore. Ronald and Connie appeared in the late afternoon and made dinner, bustling about in the small kitchen while the children stayed put in front of the TV. 'Ronald paid,' she admonished.

The children responded: 'Thank you.'

'That's not necessary, Connie,' he laughed. He made two Bloody Marys at his house bar.

'Isn't Ronald a wonderful father?' Connie called. 'He even knows how to play baseball! He really does!'

The children totalled up the benefits: baseball, steaks for dinner, a television treated like a close friend, not an enemy or someone you refused to see for a year to express mourning. And Connie was so relaxed and happy, the bathroom had toilet-paper with flowers on it – 'Yes, I saw that and had to have it. It's new on the market.' And Dicker spoke his judgement, in a loud voice, squeaky with worry.

'If you remarry, you'll be excommunicated you know.'

After dinner, Ronald turned the TV back on, and when everyone was engrossed in a murder story he settled down in his easy chair with a good book on just-war theory.

Sally slipped away to see him.

'Have you found out anything?'

'I'm working on it.' He no longer considered this an appropriate pursuit for an eight-year-old girl. 'You stop worrying and enjoy life,' he said. 'I want you to put it out of your mind entirely.' She looked at his eyes, then at his forehead transected by that deep parallel line. The skin of his face was otherwise soft and unwrinkled. She stood before him, her belly hanging out slightly, and examined his rough upper lip, the glimmer of his teeth, the round lower lip, then his pointy chin. She admired his large, hard Adam's apple. Finally she took his hand and kissed it. She whispered, 'I can't stand the thought of living another minute with him. I want to move back to our father's house. But not without my mother either. I want us to be together. The way we were. I hate my grandfather. He made everything go wrong.'

Ronald flushed. He tousled the child's blonde hair, tweaked her flat nose, passed over the red mouth to tap her chin. 'You're missing a murder out there.' He knew he was doing the right thing, keeping her out of this dirty business. She had not a clue about theology.

He realized he could no longer avoid talking openly to Connie. She must help. She was, possibly, the only one who would tell him the truth. He resolved to speak to Connie the very next time they went down into the tunnels.

9

After the Bauer family returned to their home in Palmerston North, Dr Ronald Hake resumed his studies deep in the night, in the City Morgue. The heating had been restored by the evening, and gradually the rooms warmed up enough for him to take off his winter coat, and then his sweater. He sat at his desk, the picture of Carl Bauer lying in front of him, and he observed with remorse that the man had a beatific expression on his face, obviously directed to the trees, and to his granddaughter. The photo was dusty. He spat on it and wiped the photo with his sleeve.

He remembered his lesson of first-year tissue pathology: intuition is of great usefulness in evaluating evidence. However, intuition alone will not lead to a desired degree of diagnostic accuracy. The analysis of evidence is incomplete if one is left only with the vague notion that a trait looks 'bad' or 'ugly' or 'malignant'. The final interpretation must be formed by verbalized application of the criteria. Use of the criteria should allow one to *comfortably* classify a benign or malignant trait as a specific category, for example repair, grade-one squamous, cell carcinoma, or grade-four adenocarcinoma.

Dr Hake remembered the handkerchief with the initials E.B. and thought, how touching that one should take one's best handkerchiefs along on an immigration. He looked at the photo. Carl Bauer's secret looked bad, ugly, but not malignant. And what did analysis show?

Dr Hake came to a conclusion.

A diagnosis was simple. Carl Bauer was cured of being Adolf Hitler. Adolf Hitler no longer existed. He had withdrawn ever more from the person of Carl Bauer, becoming a secret.

He had shrunk.

Hitler was a benign tumour inside Carl Bauer.

The best he could do was write the whole thing up as a biopsy report.

That same night, he again set pen to paper.

Clinical history.

Seventy-one-year-old man with well-defined secret pressing on his nerves, causing biliousness of disposition and a jaundiced view of politics. The patient suffers bouts of apathy, and unhappiness, but is otherwise able to lead a normal life, attending weekly mass, taking the sacraments, and he appears to be in a state of grace.

Gross description.

The secret was identified and labelled Adolf Hitler by an alert granddaughter. The specimen appears grossly free of sin. The mass of lie is fairly well circumscribed with ideas of German-Aryan origin, containing multiple foci of necrotic hatreds. Nazi pigment on most beliefs including his total acceptance of God. Only his love of America shows no obvious infiltration.

The neo-plasm is encapsulated by piety. This pseudo-capsule may keep the tumour from becoming invasive again.

Therapy.

It would be ill advised to slice through pseudo-capsule, piety, in order to study the secret, because this could activate the tumour. The medical problem is unique: on a deceased man, you can inspect a tumour. But in this case, the tumour will disappear at the very instant that consciousness is lost.

Dr Hake considered his report finished and he didn't know what to do with it. He regretted that he didn't have a single quote from the patient or his family to use as support. He guessed that one other person might definitely know Carl Bauer's secret: Stanislav Reich. A Jew, Connie's husband would possibly have more of an interest in talking about his father-in-law's past.

The thought of Connie's husband holding the key to his research annoyed Ronald. He began to sweat. He wondered whether he could be coming down with a viral infection. He opened his collar, and unbuttoned his shirt. His shirt was drenched. Then he realized that the room was unbearably hot. He opened his office door and noted that the hall was no cooler. The morgue had a fever.

When Dr Hake left the morgue, it was already day, and a light flurry of snow blew along the streets. On his way he passed Father Fowler's church, and on impulse he went to the front door and tried the door handle. He was relieved that the church was open. He entered, dipped his hand into the holy water and made a sign of the cross. The drops caught in the deep fold on his forehead as if it were a gutter, and gathered there, finally spilling out at either side, running down his cheeks like tears.

He brushed his face with his palms, selected a middle pew, and got down on his knees. Shyly at first, then with more force, he asked the Lord for forgiveness that he could not believe. The organization that could cure Adolf Hitler, turning a despicable tyrant into a gentleman without any due process of law, was worthy of more respect than he could accord it. 'I believe only what I see, but perhaps that is wrong of me.'

In the dimly lit church, Ronald could just make out his damp hands. They were stronger, heavier, than they had been the last time he saw them folded in the steeple position. He had been a teenager. For the first time in his adult life, Ronald considered that he, Dr Ronald Hake, might be a pious man. It was a trial run, an introspection. And he liked what he saw.

Meanwhile, something curious was going on in Palmerston North.

'Your grandfather has a sister,' said Gerda to the children when she woke them up in the morning. 'Now hurry up and get dressed.'

'What! He has a what?'

'A sister.'

'What's her name?'

'Bertha.'

'How old is she? We want to see her.'

'Not such a fuss, please.'

'She's your aunt,' said Connie, coming into their room, sleepy and matronly for once. She sat down on Sally's camp-bed, and stroked Sally's hair. 'Your great-aunt. She lives very far away. In Argentina. But she's coming to see us. You should play the violin for her, Sally. Can you arrange a programme?'

They couldn't imagine Opa having any relatives. On the way home from school Gerda said, 'Your aunt is coming

116

to visit us for an hour tomorrow. Don't talk about religion with your aunt.'

Not talk about religion?

They let it slide past.

The next day, driving them to school, Connie said, 'Your aunt is coming this afternoon. Don't talk to her about religion please.'

They asked why, and she replied, 'Some people don't like to talk about it. But you can play the violin for her.'

Not talk about it?

But the whole point of religion was to talk about it.

'Don't talk about religion with your great-aunt, her name is Bertha, by the way,' Connie said. For two days Connie talked and talked about not talking about religion. 'Call her Aunt Bertha. She's coming all the way from Argentina. That's where she lives. Because she wants to see your grandfather. Don't talk to her about religion. Religion is a private matter.'

'We can't wait to talk to Aunt Bertha about her relationship to God!' said Sally, sly as always. 'Or is that religion too?'

'It is, and you damn well know it,' replied Connie.

'Tell them, Connie,' Gerda said, interfering.

'Yes, their manners are too awful to be reliable. Little savages. OK, listen, children: don't talk to Aunt Bertha about religion because she's sensitive about it, and that's final.'

'What does sensitive mean?'

'She's not Catholic.'

'Not Catholic!'

'That's right. Now you know. Sally, you could play a Beethoven sonatina for her. No church music.'

'What is she then, if she's not Catholic?'

'She's Jewish. Jew-ish. There. She happens to have converted to Judaism. She decided that she believes in Judaism, the way you believe in Catholicism. That's all. Now please don't discuss it with her. We've talked enough about it, and I expect not to hear another word about the matter.'

The aunt was arriving that afternoon. Connie said she was a simple, good-natured soul whose life ambition was to see Disneyland. She had a stop-over in New York, no more than that. She wasn't really going to have time to see her brother either. But she didn't know that yet.

'He doesn't want to see her,' Gerda said. She sounded annoyed.

'If we converted to Judaism he wouldn't want to see us either,' said Sally. 'What's so good-natured about converting to Judaism? Whoooey!'

When Connie went to pick up Aunt Bertha, Sally and Dicker discussed the matter. Sister Mary Angela had been most lucid on the subject. If you died as an unbaptized baby: limbo. But if you died knowing you could be Catholic instead: hell for ever. The children could hardly wait for their aunt's arrival. They had never met someone who was going to hell, with absolute certainty, barring a last-minute reconversion.

When they heard Connie's car rattle up to the house, the children hid behind the curtain of the porch window. From there they watched an elderly woman, dressed much too coolly for November, proceed up the front walk. She smiled anxiously, as if she knew someone might be watching her. And they could not stop staring at her body, at those wispy arms and legs, the powdered skin on her face and neck and her sparse white hair, because they saw the flames of hell already licking at them.

After shaking hands, the children retreated to their room and tried not to think about the visitor. They heard the drone of female voices downstairs – at one point, it seemed to them that the aunt might be crying; there was some spluttering and a sharp protest involving the name 'Mein Carl'. Then Sally was called. Sally took her fiddle and went downstairs, while Dicker stayed put. Soon the chorale of the Ninth Symphony racked the house. Happy came whining upstairs, and Dicker took him into bed, and put his pillow over their ears. Sally never returned upstairs. She stayed with the grown-ups for the entire afternoon, and listened to them talk about the weather in Argentina. Aunt Bertha called her the politest grand-niece anyone could have wished. Neither the visitor nor Sally ever mentioned religion once, and even Gerda, who was given to candour at the wrong moments, maintained a respectful silence on the matter.

First thing in the morning, Dr Hake had a Mafia shoot-out victim. He looked for bullets with the enthusiasm of an adult hunting for Easter eggs. He was bored and preoccupied. He went to the men's room and had a word with himself in the mirror. He argued:

– Go on then, Ronald, you must have a definite answer. Be a hero. Make that phone call.

– But I'd make a fool of myself.

Dr Hake hadn't fought in the Second World War, the way Dr Guttenberg had, who battled with his boredom at cocktail parties by describing submarine warfare. Dr Miele had been a medic in Korea, while Dr Hake enjoyed a medical-school deferment. It wasn't Dr Hake's fault that the war ended before he could enlist. He had never really had the chance to prove himself.

Dr Miele emerged from a stall and watched Dr Hake conducting a silent conversation with his reflection.

There are other forms of heroism. Dr Hake has dedicated his life to knowledge, and is willing to risk all: he will put his dignity on the block.

Dr Miele shook his head in wonder, and pushed past Dr Hake.

'You holding on to your sanity OK, Donalronal?'

'My sanity is scarcely at risk,' Dr Hake answered coldly. The thought of the mental-ward patients banging their cups made him hesitate. But then he clinched the argument, as the bathroom door swung shut behind Dr Miele.

– Forget your pride, forget the nature of the relationship, boyfriend/husband.

He left the bathroom and dialled the number. 'Dr Reich, please.'

The Nobel Prize-winner's secretary had just walked in the door. She needed to put on her comfortable shoes and see what her boss was doing. 'Professor Stanislav Reich?' she said. 'Mmmmm.' She put her pumps under the desk. 'Professor Reich is at a meeting and I can't possibly disturb him. Your name?'

Ronald was too proud to leave his name with a secretary. He shoved his post back in the refrigerator and sprinted to the uptown bus.

Stanislav was a member of a distinguished, poorly paid faculty of science. The university had cleaned up during the war on freshly immigrated Jewish scientists grateful for subsistence wages. Given the chance to pick their own technicians, these refugees surrounded themselves with staff from the same obscure neck of the woods. The secretaries spoke the best English in the building. As Ronald neared Dr Reich's laboratory, he heard furious Polish voices.

Ronald tracked them, thus avoiding the secretary, who was staying out of this. He recognized Stanislav Reich from the newspapers, standing in a circle of three Polish technicians, all with wide faces, bleached blonde hair, short heavy legs, and, at the moment, one opinion. Dr Reich was stuck in the middle. It looked like an uncomfortable fit. The group noticed Ronald's entrance but did not stop haranguing Stanislav. Finally, Stanislav put his hands in front of himself as if he were pushing open a door, whipped the technicians aside and proceeded towards the newcomer.

Ronald felt the deflation of his Yale MD in the presence of this Nobel Prize-winner, a real researcher, not a plain little medical man. 'Dr Hake,' he said, 'a Princeton biologist, Yale Medical Doctor. I wanted to talk to you about Connie.'

'About Connie!' The word Connie was picked up at once and tossed around by the Polish women behind Stanislav.

'Stach,' one finally said, 'as your oldest friends in the world, we've always stayed with you, although you're an awful boss, inconsiderate, never remember a birthday the way you're supposed to here, still we beg you: go back to her. You're a mess. Who cares about this Nobel thing? Your clothes, Stanislav. Come on, Bronya, Wanda, let's go. The gentleman probably has a message from that foolish little wife of his. Such a shirt he wears, expects us to work for him, the secretary doesn't care what he looks like because he's the big man now, and he walks around with oatmeal on his vest.'

'Stanislav, goodbye. We finish the DNA reaction now.'

They pecked him on the cheek.

'Go back to her.'

'Be a good boy.'

'Your mother would scream. I can hear her.'

'If she weren't dead.'

'Death spared her.'

They fluttered out. Stanislav sighed. He didn't look at Ronald. 'What can I do for you?' he said.

He turned around and walked out of the room. Ronald followed him. Stanislav settled into his pace position, head down slightly, back hunched, fingers twiddling a plastic spoon behind his back. He ran up and down the hall like that. Ronald had to strain to keep up with him while trying to find his voice.

Suddenly Stanislav stopped short. He looked at his cheap watch. 'Time for lunch. I'm going to the cafeteria if you care to join me.'

They proceeded without talking down several flights of stairs and corridors to the doctors' cafeteria. Stanislav went through the queue without looking at Ronald, considering for a long time before taking a 'long-life plate'. Then he grabbed an extra helping of napkins and remarked, 'I forgot to buy Kleenex.'

He paid for himself, and sat down at a window seat.

He ate like a garbage truck. Ronald was overcome with sympathy that Connie had been forced to share so many years of her life with someone who had such bad manners.

'Dr Reich, I've come about Connie,' he finally ventured.

Stanislav looked up briefly, and spoke, his mouth full. 'About my wife.'

'Yes. I'm a colleague of hers at the City Hospital –'

'Oh, you're one of those carrion doctors,' said Stanislav. He sat back, swallowed, and glared at Ronald's hands, obviously wondering whether he had washed them after handling contagious tissue.

'I'm worried about her father.'

'Pardon me? What has her father to do with your job? He's not dead yet, is he?'

'If he were, I wouldn't have these worries. No. I need your help. You know the Bauer family very well.'

'I do, yes,' said Stanislav. 'I am going to have a pastry now. Excuse me. They're excellent. And inexpensive.'

He stood up and headed towards the queue again. After a while he returned with a large chunk of cream cake, and more napkins. 'This is on the house. I didn't have to pay one penny for this. Because of my Nobel Prize. You know I just won the Nobel Prize!' He ate with relish. The whipped cream landed on his chin and hung there.

'Have you noticed that Connie's father is anti-Semitic?' asked Ronald.

'You mean he doesn't like Jews? But that's very normal for his generation of Germans,' said Stanislav.

'I'm not sure it's so normal.'

'What do you want from me?' asked Stanislav. 'Do you have a message from my wife? Or what? You don't come here to talk to me about Connie's father. I don't understand. He's ill, I know, I haven't visited him. I hate hospitals.' He looked like he was shaving.

'Let's talk about your daughter, Sally,' began Ronald. 'I might add, a darling, clever child. She's asked me for

123

help. She thinks that your father-in-law might have been a very bad Nazi back in Germany.'

'A bad Nazi?'

Ronald allowed himself to laugh, a coughed chuckle, bringing up revelation. 'Yes, in fact, she suspects the worst, really. A man who committed a great many crimes. A real Führer. In fact – '

'I don't want to talk to you any more,' said Stanislav. He stood up from the table, abandoning his cake. 'Who are you, anyway? Connie's colleague? Disgusting. You're a snoop.'

He repeated this loudly, to all the distinguished professors in the cafeteria, in his Polish accent. 'Deżgustiç. Jórę Snóp.'

10

The priest asked all the boys from the middle grades to assemble in the front hall before lessons started. They stood in a disorderly circle around him and waited for the special thing he had to tell them.

'Boys,' he said. 'Some parents have brought it to my attention that their sons are not making a complete confession, that they're leaving out

'a mortal sin,

'which means that their souls are not clean when they go to communion!

'Now, boys, I've noticed that some of you do have a lot of trouble confessing

'a certain sin

'to me. And I've decided that it's in the interest of Our Lord to make it easier for you to talk about

'this sin, the sin' –

he paused; their hearts raced in fear and shame –

'of impurity.'

General blushing. The priest too.

'From now on, boys, when you want to talk about impurity to me, you may just use the word "Shark". I will know what you're talking about. Is that clear? Shark. I think this will make things a lot easier.'

'Shark,' the boys mumbled to themselves, practising. 'Shark,' 'Shark.'

PJ had never been invited to see the Bauers' bedroom. She glanced at the plain pine wardrobe, the prayer stool, the cheap Persian carpet on the floor, the clock on the wall. It wasn't very attractive. She looked balefully at the bed. It was very wide. Eva had insinuated once, in a flash of trust when the two women were waiting for Carl to use a rest room in Strasbourg, that she had not exactly enjoyed sleeping with her husband. All those years, he had insisted, she had complied. She had not put it that way. She had said – PJ recalled the stinging words exactly – 'Carl always likes to you-know on vacations. I get so tired of it. I need my sleep more than he does.'

At least the Bauer bed had two blankets and two pillows. One pillow had Eva's photo propped up on it, the other was plumped and ready for use. A prayer book and rosary lay on the bedside table.

PJ lay down on Carl's side. She felt herself sink into the worn mattress and knew how shiny and black her hair must look against the white pillow to any observer. In this case, to Eva. With her right hand, she flipped Eva's photograph on its back. That's how it had been: Eva had turned her face into the pillow, while Carl had lain with her. The beds had been uncomfortable, French. Impossible sausage pillows. He had performed, goodness me, and how. Power, power, power. Eva was probably peeking the whole time, her head tucked down into the pillow. It obviously didn't matter to her at all. She didn't complain. A perversion. It qualified. No, wait a minute. PJ struggled with herself. She was getting fact and fantasy mixed up. It hadn't come to *that*.

126

PJ remembered very clearly how they had run into each other in the bathroom between their hotel suites. Both naked. He wouldn't let her see him. He sidled out of the bathroom back into his suite. It was charming, really. She wouldn't let him see her either.

That morning in Strasbourg had been warm and languid. The hotel had packed them a picnic lunch. All this French food. 'Isn't my ancestral town dandy?' PJ said. 'Now let's go and see yours. It's right over the river. We can just stroll.'

'But neither of us were born here,' said Eva.

'We come from Austria, you know.'

PJ wanted that cuckoo clock. She had led them through the airy woods that ran along the river. She felt as if she knew the place, even though she didn't speak a word of French. That was heritage. With a reliable instinct that came partly from consulting a map available at the hotel reception desk, she brought them all the way to the bridge without ever leaving the protection of the trees. They didn't suspect a thing; their feet trod softly, willingly, on the warm earth until they turned up another path ('Look! Let's go this way and see what happens!') which brought them quite suddenly out of the woods, into the clearing, into the bright sunlight reflecting off the river, so that it took a few seconds for one's eyes to adjust, and then they saw they were looking right up the bridge, to the border crossing at the far end.

'Come on, kids! Let's cross,' she said.

Eva had collapsed. Her legs simply gave way. PJ, lying on Carl's bed, flipped over on her belly, and began petting the hard back of Eva's photo. She had looked like a beached whale. In a floral dress. Carl massaging her chubby fins. He had looked so unhappy that PJ had

127

been forced to leave Eva lying there, in order to attend first to the shocked husband.

That night Carl had told PJ that Eva was evidently ill. He was going to take her home. Six years later, PJ flopped over and drowned in Carl's pillow, whimpering at the memory. Then she heard the car roll up in front of the house. PJ scurried to the window and saw the taxi, the driver helping Carl out of the back seat. She did not hurry off, she had a desire to be found out, but Gerda and Carl were slow. By the time they had helped each other up the front stairs, PJ had slipped out of the back door, deposited the key in its rightful place underneath the bin, and was percolating coffee in her kitchen. 'I could have robbed them. But I didn't!' she said to herself. 'Ex-Lutherans have principles too.' It was just as well. She had reached the end of the journey in her memory. The Bauers had taken the next train back to Cherbourg. PJ had refused to give them their boat tickets, so he had paid for new ones himself. They were forced to travel the lowest class, the poor things.

Carl Bauer entered the house and the clocks chimed, and their hands saluted. The checker sets waited, spit and polished, the armies entrenched in their positions; they hadn't moved without their commander. The dog exhausted himself wagging his old tail. The plastic recliner stood straight-backed proclaiming its readiness for service. The flame on Eva's candle bounced joyfully and the glass of Eva's portrait shone, so that the smile on her face looked fresh. The phone rang.

Stanislav calling. 'Oh, you are back home! How glad I am to hear that. I heard you were ill. I wanted to enquire about your condition.'

'Thank you for your curiosity,' Carl said curtly. 'How is your science?'

'Very well, very well. I wish you all the best,' Stanislav replied and hung up. No natural manners.

'It was Stanislav,' he told Gerda. 'He should mind his own business,' he said. His voice wavered audibly and she stared at him, horrified.

'Yes. He just upsets Mr Bauer, doesn't he. He shouldn't call. Always calling.'

'Did he call before?'

'I don't know. I wasn't there much. But I think so.'

'And where are the children?'

'In school, of course. I think Mr Bauer should lie down for a while.'

Ronald did not return to work. He felt a migraine coming on. He went home, stripped and hid under his own covers. After a few hours, the doorbell rang.

Connie had slipped off from the morgue to see what was the matter. 'I suddenly had the feeling you weren't well. It just came to me. You left without closing the fridge door properly and we saw it was your case. It's not like you to be messy. I couldn't concentrate any more, I was so worried. Isn't that funny? Telepathy.'

His headache disappeared. He undressed her and then he made love to her with all the passion stirred up by the shame of being treated condescendingly by her husband. Afterwards, his self-confidence was restored. He knew that Stanislav couldn't ever pull off the same performance. He suddenly had an idea – how to get to the bottom of the mystery once and for all. Connie was dozing next to him. He woke her gently and said, 'I

129

want to ask you to marry me. But before I ask you, I want you to tell me your family history.'

He said it that simply, and it made eminent sense to him, the son of a Greenwich big businessman, to enquire about his future bride's background.

Connie lay still. Her body and her face did not register the slightest surprise, either at the marriage proposal or at the request for family credentials. She stayed where she was, huddling in his arms (he did not remove them, so he could feel her body temperature as she talked; he'd catch any change of texture – sweating or trembling – when she entered that colourful cluttered landscape of deceit). The fact that she was undressed would not make her more honest, Ronald thought. To the contrary, she'll use it to conceal things, pushing up against me at certain places in the story, as though this might distract me.

'I have news for you: I'm descended from Russian nobility.'

'Why didn't you tell me before?' asked Ronald, not believing a word of it.

'I didn't want to make you envious,' she said.

'Their titles?'

'I can't remember. What's so important about a title, anyway?'

'They come first. Start with their title. You said they have one.'

'Count Bauer.'

A few seconds after saying it, she giggled, and although he did not respond in kind, she embarked with enthusiasm on her story.

'In the 1800s my mother's ancestor, a man called something like Kisselov, fled some Cossack rebellion on a white horse. He crossed the swamps and the back-waters all the way to the Danube. He settled in a real castle there, smugly watched the end of the Tsar and the installation of someone no better at all, and after a fair amount of procreation, which led to intermarriage with the locals, he lived happily ever after.

'I think that was the problem: longevity wreaks havoc on families. Kisselov picked up a religious tick at sixty-five; he dressed up in rags he had fitted by his tailor and torn by his favourite bulldog; he hallucinated in the gardens; and after a conversation in the marketplace with a handsome fanatic priest, Kisselov handed over his castle to an order of friars.

'Otherwise,' said Connie, 'I'd be living in that castle today.'

'You can roll it through faster,' Ronald said, uninterested, 'if you don't even know their names. Not too many irrelevant details. I don't want to try every leaf on your path. I'm not a snail.'

'Irrelevant? What's irrelevant about being a count, darling?'

'Go on,' said Ronald. 'What happened then?'

Connie's voice trailed off. 'I'm sleepy,' she complained. 'Have I bored you, you poor thing? And I thought as an American you'd like to hear I had a castle in my background.' She nestled next to him. Ronald shook her. She opened her eyes, made a feeble attempt at seduction. He pushed her away slightly, and looked stern. 'Now you know everything,' she complained. 'What else do you want to know?'

'Begin with your grandparents,' Ronald said.

She was silent.

'My guess is your family was lower middle class.

Not quite the basement. First floor, with a good view of the gutter. Maybe your grandfather was a Customs inspector, that sort of thing.'

'Worse.'

'Worse! What was his name?'

'Peter Bauer.'

'And what did he do?'

'He was an artist. I called him Opa Peter. He was a specialized kind of photographer. My father had a hard time living up to his reputation. He travelled all through Europe from the Alps to the Baltic, and made family portraits for the peasants with his special camera. They would put on their Sunday best, all twenty or thirty of them, and smile formally for an hour while he fidgeted around underneath the camera curtain. They pooled together their money, paid him, and he left to develop the picture. I adored Opa Peter. They never saw him again. He had no film in the camera.'

'Oh Christ.'

'He was lovely. My father was terribly embarrassed about him. My mother wouldn't let me sit on his lap as a child because she thought I'd catch a disease. She came from a much finer family. Really, a fine family.'

'What did they do?'

She stopped. He waited. After a while she said, 'I don't remember.'

'Your mother's maiden name?'

'I don't know any more. Do you actually remember your grandmother's family name?'

'Coombs.'

'Oh, Coooooombs,' she imitated.

'Right. Silent B after the M.'

'Well, all of my grandmother's name is silent.'

132

Ronald persisted. 'What was your mother's father like? You must remember that.'

'Short. Bald. Very religious.'

'And your grandmother, his wife?'

'A mother. Strong. The women were strong in that family, and always being disappointed by their husbands. My family personified the disappointment between the sexes.' He permitted her to try to change the subject. 'Men want to have a strong mother, and women want to have a strong knight. Haven't you ever noticed that strong mothers are more common than strong knights?'

'What's that supposed to mean! Did she have lots of children? Then your father would have had many cousins. Can you remember any of your aunts and uncles?'

'Oh dear, I can't answer all these questions. I have a weak memory for names and faces. I may forget you tomorrow.'

'Because I'm asking you these questions? Darling, come on,' he said urgently. 'Get it over with. I want to know. I'd like to marry you. Those are things we ask in this country.'

'I should get back to work now,' she said, sitting up. 'I'm afraid I have to disappoint you. I don't remember a damn thing.'

She settled on the word 'damn' hard, and it shocked him, a woman being vulgar. 'OK then,' he said.

'You know everything that's important,' she said.

'I don't.'

'What don't you know?'

'Why you left Austria.'

'Because we robbed a bank and the sheriff said we had to be out of there by sundown.'

133

He looked at her with disgust, wondering what gave her the right to sit on his bed.

'I don't know why. One day my parents packed their bags, and we left.'

'When was it, what year?'

'It was just after the war.'

'You told me once it was before the war!'

'Did I? I wasn't thinking.'

'And why did they leave? Austria's a nice place, mountain scenery, old churches, real cuisine. They must have had a good reason to leave.'

'I never asked. I was a very polite child, I never questioned my parents. I let them pack. And then they sent me to Gerda's house for a few days. Gerda is the maid you met. Gerda had a little cottage on a mountain.'

'Like Heidi.'

'Exactly like Heidi.'

'And you never asked why. How romantic.'

'Well, yes, I did, after a few days there, I did ask why were my parents packing, what was going on. She was very annoyed at me.

'"Don't be a rabbit," she said to me. She grasped my shoulder' – Connie grasped her bare shoulder – 'like this, with her rough hand, and she kept snarling at me, "A scared little bunny rabbit," and then she shook me and shook me and shook me. "They're going to America."'

After this last sentence, Connie lay down again and broke into tears. Tears of fatigue, thought Ronald. He could not get another word out of her. The pillow became sodden. He held her, still nursing the hope that the truth might wash out with the tears. But she refused to say another word. She's just invented a family, thought Ronald, it's no surprise she's exhausted.

Then he marvelled at the quality of her invention, and decided, evasive people probably tell the best stories, that's why I hate novels, just one big ugly piece of self-deception, never read the damn things.

Hours later, Dr Hake became furious. She was just an ordinary liar. The whole family. Liars. Living off the fat of the land. Maggots. Digesting facts, excreting fiction. And she thought she was going to marry him. Why wouldn't she just come out and tell him the truth? The Church is very clear on the question of lying – when it harms the dignity of others, then it is a sin. And this is harming my dignity.

Connie had gone back to work, bearing the news that Dr Hake had a fierce migraine and wouldn't be in again. Dr Guttenberg wanted to know how Dr Bauer had managed to acquire this knowledge. She said Hake had called and asked her to bring him some medicine, and she had brought him the medicine. Dr Guttenberg said, 'Was he in bed?' and Dr Bauer chuckled and said, 'Honestly, Dr Guttenberg. I didn't check. I rang the bell and left it standing outside his door. I didn't want to disturb him in his silk pyjamas, you know? He won't be inventing a migraine, if that's what you're concerned about.'

'Silk pyjamas you see through the door?'

At that moment, Dr Hake was entering Precinct 109 of the Manhattan Police. He had on his clinician's white jacket now, and looked as respectable as any doctor. He was very grim and composed, unlike most people reporting a crime, and asked to see the head of the Precinct.

Officer Ignatius had his mind occupied with the bomber. He didn't want to be disturbed. But the junior officer said he'd better have a word with the doctor; he was a forensic pathologist, and it was a tip-off. Nevertheless, Ignatius treated the doctor disparagingly. He didn't believe much in tip-offs. He had heard a lot about them in his forty years of service, without ever experiencing a useful one. Mostly they were lies and rumours and he treated them with a simple routine: he turned them over to the Press. The Press was reliable. The Press got to the bottom of the matter.

Dr Hake stressed confidentiality. 'I don't want any official investigation. I just want some help.' He laid his reports on the table. The policeman glanced at the stationery, New York City Morgue. Some sort of diagnosis of Adolf Hitler, in impossible medical language. These doctors had ideas. He said, 'Write down the fellow's name and address, please.' He shoved a form in the doctor's direction.

Dr Hake printed, in big letters. Then he attended to his pipe, which impressed the cop (skilful bastard, the way he loads it, tamps it and gets it going). The police officer stared at the pipe, at the form, his hand settled over the telephone as he observed the first puff of smoke sail into the room and, without looking, he dialled a number. Like a pianist who knows a piece, the cop had the number in his huge red forefinger. 'Mr Parker?' he asked. 'Jim Ignatius. We have a report here of a fellow who may be Adolf Hitler. Yep, that's right, the dictator, the German fellow. He's supposed to be dead – right, everyone knows he's probably around. Try the old guy at' (he squinted at the form) 'twelve-zero-seven River Avenue. In Palmerston North, right over the bridge.

Makes sense. You fellows will find out everything faster than we can.'

When he hung up, Dr Hake was looking askance at him. 'Who was that?'

'The *Amercian Inquirer*, Doc. They'll find out everything you want to know within a few hours.'

Dr Hake cursed and went out.

11

The first two reporters had no problem finding the house. Red-brick row house, the perfect location for someone to hide. They had a good look at it, and rang the doorbell. Gerda answered.

'Mr Bauer is sick in bed. What do you want?' She was hostile.

'Just some questions, Mrs, ah . . .'

'Miss Schmidt.'

'Miss Schmidt, can you just tell us where Mr Bauer comes from? Is he German?'

'No, of course not. What do you want from Mr Bauer?'

They retreated before she could get angry.

'Denies he's German.'

'So what's she going to say!'

'Forget this. We have to ask the neighbours.'

The neighbours were already on the way. PJ had spent the morning primping. It was December. It was Wednesday. It was The Day. This time, she was going to go in the front door. First ring, then go in. She was wearing a simple dress, nothing extravagant, green as the lawn overlooking the Rhine, and no more make-up than a touch of lipstick, and a good perfume. It had cost her nerves. Eighteen months of waiting. She could tell you a thing or two about suffering for love.

'May we ask your name?'

'Patricia June De Ville,' she answered. 'I bet you're interviewing about brand preferences. Boy, this is my day. Do we get free samples?'

'No, no, ma'am. Brad is my name. This is Jeff. We're just making a few enquiries about your neighbour here. We may write something about him. Ah, there's some rumours going around, maybe you can tell us about them . . .'

Her face turned so white it disappeared, leaving her red mouth. They were going to ask her about a woman who'd been seen breaking and entering the Bauer home and not taking anything. They must want to know what that burglar was doing in there. She started to turn around and run off, thought better of it, and snapped, 'Stupid rumours, I bet. Rumours have never ever interested me in the very merry ordinary slightest. So there.'

'We've heard that this fellow living here, Mr Carl Bauer, is a German. Is that true?'

She stopped mentally in her tracks. Curiosity began to sniff inside her like a dog. 'German? Why, yes, he's – no, he's not, in fact he's very particular about that: don't make that mistake. He's Austrian. Which isn't the same a'tall. Now don't you boys ask me why. I've never been. We went to France together. Him, his wife, now passed away, God *bless* her. But not to Germany. He didn't want to. If you ask me, he panicked. You know, a little fear about going back there. Ya, he's sort of German. I don't know.'

She looked the two men over. Well dressed, serious looking. 'Why do you ask?'

They shifted from foot to foot. It was cold out there. Finally the taller one, named Brad, said, 'Look, we're just

139

checking out a rumour, making sure it's no more than that. They say this fellow might be Hitler, you know? Adolf Hitler. Now, do you know him well?'

PJ stared into the cold. Then a sound began in her chest, a rumble, a groan, she pursed her lips and it came out 'oo oo oo' and she began to rock her head forwards and backwards.

'That's all right, lady, take it easy,' the reporters said. Brad put his arm around her shoulder. 'There's got to be something to this, all right,' he said to his colleague. 'Come on, lady, I'll bring you home.'

Dicker was having his obesity class, Sally a violin lesson. Fate had obviously laid its plans carefully. The journalists converged on a nearly empty house. The photographers came and staked out the entrances in case he tried to get away. The neighbours trickled together slowly. Brad returned from PJ's house and said, 'I got some great quotes about their trip to Europe. She says him being Hitler explains everything. She's had a shock. She's packing to go to her son's house, out in Tucson. But she gave me the address there in case we need her.'

Inside the house, Happy was getting nervous. He kept poking his nose at Gerda's legs and whining. She rapped him on the nose several times and concentrated on dinner. She was cooking dumplings to welcome him home.

Upstairs, Carl was supposed to be in bed, but a man has to go to the toilet. When he looked out of the bathroom window, he saw the crowd. He came downstairs, slowly, quietly, in his bathrobe and slippers. He made it to Connie's porch without Gerda noticing. He peered through the curtains. One of the photographers was waiting for that. The light flashed, a burst of light into that dark house. 'Hey,' a journalist screamed, 'here's Hitler!'

140

They managed several good shots of the face peering out between gauze porch curtains, the round blue eyes, the quaint Hitler moustache, the red cheeks.

Carl Bauer felt driven by doom. He approached the front door. Now Gerda heard him and, dropping her last dumpling into the water, hurried to see what he was up to. He threw open the door before she could stop him. Ten lights went off in his face: Hitler in his bathrobe and slippers, his stature hasn't changed a bit, sure, it's him. Look at that moustache.

Carl turned back as the reporters surged up the stairs. He slammed the door in their faces, but not before Happy had slipped through and was making one great nuisance of himself, snarling and snapping. Meanwhile, his master sagged, he wilted, he withered. He said, 'Please, Almighty God. Show me thy intentions.' Perhaps God doesn't like theories about himself and the revelation of his intentions. The life force let Carl Bauer die, in the hands of his maid, while Happy was ineffectually trying to save his honour.

The paper went to press that evening. It was on the newsstands the next sunny and seasonally cold morning. 'HITLER FOUND IN PALMERSTON NORTH!' The Yuletide raged in the shop windows. Ronald saw the headlines on his way to work. He stopped on the street, stood stiff and still, his lips twitching with inner monologue, just like all the other nuts, while the pedestrians pushed past him. But in his case it was only an attack of pride. Acute self-satisfaction works like bronchio-constriction, causing pressure in the chest, pounding in the ears, brain-swelling, followed after a few minutes by rapid jerks of the limbs – he ran for the bus. Back to the suburbs. Through Harlem, where no one cared about the news, to the stettl where

141

no one bothered to read English papers. Ronald arrived at the house on River Avenue while the reporters were still recovering from a long night of writing. Gerda had strung Christmas lights on the dogwood tree in front. He rang the bell – sure is a beautiful morning. He was fierce with courage: I shall now sort this thing out once and for all, I read the paper this morning! Amazing news! He was going to play modest, and not admit he was responsible for the *in vivo* discovery.

Gerda told him about the death at the door. She wore parson's black, but her face was matter of fact, as if she was immune to grief. She wasn't surprised to see him, either, allowed him in, and cared where he sat. 'Sit anywhere but in Mr Bauer's recliner. Connie's coming back. She's at the funeral home.' She stood in front of the recliner to make sure he wouldn't dare occupy it. He sat on the pioneer sofa, and his gaze turned automatically to the television, tunnel entrance to the American psyche. Still dark. Two candles flickered on top. A copy of the *American Inquirer* lay on the pine coffee table. The visitor picked it up and held it to his eyes. 'Someone stuffed it through the mail slot. Probably PJ,' Gerda said, still hovering in front of the recliner, in case the visitor changed his mind.

'And what do you think of it?' he asked. He expected denials, the lies of the primitive. She stared at him, her beak opening and shutting. She stuttered, and when the words finally came out, her mouth hammered the vowels. 'Wh-wh-wh-wh-when, when they went to America, I taught them. I taught them how to pray. You put your han-han-hands like this, I said, I showed them. I told them about co-o-o-mmunion, Jesus, the Host. I taught them everything. Baptism by desire. They're very good Catholics. The best Catholics I eee-, I eee-, I eeever knew.'

142

She sat down in the recliner herself, fluffed down into it, wide, brooding. She did not take her eyes off him. He looked at his hands, admired his own blue blood that ran up from the wrist bone to the long fingers. They sat in silence. She didn't respond when Connie and the children entered the house. Perhaps she was hard of hearing, and the recliner had its back to the door. Connie came in, appraised Ronald but said nothing. She went to Gerda, bent over and kissed her with a tenderness so odd, so wounded, so shipwrecked, and dragged up from the bottom of some ocean of feeling where it had been trapped for decades. And this tenderness was altogether unfamiliar to Ronald, and made him bitter: it was a love she had never felt for him.

Sally and Dicker said nothing. They looked watchful and dull-witted, as if they'd given up trying to make sense of a situation, but were automatically continuing to collect any relevant data. Connie sat down on the arm of the recliner, so that the stuffing squealed. She stretched her hands out, and even Dicker allowed his mother to pull him into her lap, while Sally, imitating Connie, sat down on the other arm of the chair. When the whole family had settled like that on Carl Bauer's recliner, they stared at Ronald. Connie spoke.

'I have something to tell my children. And you may listen.'

And she told them her family history with affection and familiarity until the characters, called back as spirits by recollection, seemed to join them in the living room. Connie allowed them to speak, prompting them like a souffleur.

They came, in order of disappearance.

The first to have gone was Peter Bauer, Carl Bauer's

143

father, wearing his artist's costume, baggy shirt and trousers and a beret. He was already seventy, a jovial, untroubled version of his son, when he was arrested after one of his escapades.

He'd been commissioned to make a family portrait for the mayor of a small neighbouring town. He absconded with the money. It was just after the Anschluss; they didn't fool around with petty criminals then, especially if they were Jewish.

'Yes, Jewish,' Connie repeated, as her grandfather waltzed about the living room showing not the slightest consternation about the mess he'd gotten himself into.

Then came Eva's father, clutching his Bible. He was short, bald, religious, just as Connie had once described him to Ronald. He was a Rabbi, Rabbi Breslauer. He had the bearing of an important man, he always seemed to be looking over a crowd that waited for him to speak. But it was easy to be important in Linz, especially if one came from Vienna, as he had done, to take over the synagogue.

Then came his wife, with Eva's blue eyes and blonde hair, complaining that she could not enjoy the power she exercised in the provinces because she missed the opera house in Vienna. The Breslauers appeared in fancy dress; they talked about where to hide their heirlooms and whether a well-placed friend of the family might not organize just a little salvation. They looked askance at the Bauers, who for several generations had traded in pots and pans and were next of kin with orthodox Jews from Galicia, who spoke Polish rather than German, but had somehow produced an accountant and two dentists.

'I once visited cousins in the same town where Stanislav was born,' Connie said.

When the children looked surprised, she said, 'Your father and I have that in common.' She saw they didn't understand at all, and said, 'Never mind about what we have in common.'

The spirits of the family were up on tippy-toes, trying to move without making any noise.

Connie went on. 'People are the same everywhere. Tolerance bores them. I wouldn't hold it against the Austrians. Tolerance is an awfully dull parlour game. My grandfather Breslauer kept six young men from yawning all evening. In his synagogue. They clubbed him to death.

'My family was so stupid. They thought if they didn't draw any attention to themselves, if they just didn't move a muscle, no one would notice them. But of course everyone saw them breathing.

'Whereas we had Gerda.

'Gerda persuaded my parents to leave.

'Gerda was Catholic, she knew about human meanness.'

'Don't talk like that, Connie,' Gerda interrupted.

Connie tried again. 'Gerda started out working as a housekeeper for the Breslauers in Vienna. She was violently opposed, as only someone whose opinion is not asked can be, to my mother's marriage to the son of a swindler.'

'Don't talk like that, Connie.'

'But my father won her over. He was so serious about everything, and he had his own architectural firm in Linz. When I was born, Gerda left the Rabbi's services and came to look after me.'

145

Gerda said nothing, the candles on the television flickering in her eyes.

'After my grandfather was killed in his temple, she organized baptism papers for my parents and gave us religious instruction. I remember the Sabbath afternoon, when Gerda showed us all how to make the sign of the cross. And everyone obeyed her to the letter.

'My parents left me with her when they went to Denmark. From there they made it to England, and then to America. They travelled by bribery and prayer. Aunt Bertha took different transportation on another route. When you're older I'll tell you to what lengths she went to reach Argentina.'

'Without us. Without us,' whispered the rest of the family assembled in memory only.

'I stayed with Gerda till the war ended and then we followed to America. By then, I had no one else. The others – the Bauers and the Breslauers – had no luck at all. Not one of them died of natural causes. We wanted to spare the next generation the shame of knowledge. Not all knowledge is desirable.'

Ronald Hake stood up, and the spirits scattered. Death in his suburb had been individual, competitive. He had to pass the recliner to reach the door, and Sally reached for his hand. He pulled away, his face set into an expression he hoped betrayed no shame. Just before reaching the door, he remembered the photo Sally had given him. He didn't want anything to do with it. He turned back. As he handed it to her he saw that, by spitting on the photo in order to clean it, he had ruined it. Moisture had turned everything yellow and brown. 'Sorry about that,' he remarked, and left.

It took him several hours over a suspected malpractice

146

case to decide what to do. He decided to give up women. He would have to treat Dr Bauer coolly from now on, and try to forget his error. Yes, it would become Dr Hake's own little dirty secret, swaddled in layers of piety, his pious secret.

A NOTE ON THE AUTHOR

Irene Dische is a young American living in Berlin. *Pious Secrets* introduces an original and exciting new writer.